"I'm glad you're the one assigned to find my friend's killer," Sadie said.

She bit her lip and added, "I feel safe when I'm with you." She averted her gaze as if it was too hard to see his reaction to her words.

They only served to further ignite his protectiveness.

He needed to focus. "The fact that you were abducted from her beach house and left to drown on a sinking boat suggests there must be something in this house worth looking at."

"And someone doesn't want me digging around and finding out who killed her."

A lump grew in his throat as he stared up at the beach house.

The sudden sense that someone was watching them crawled over him. Trees butted up near the house that faced the ocean. Waves crashed against the rocks behind them. Was he making a mistake?

Gage grabbed Sadie's hand and headed back toward his SUV. "This is too dangerous. I should never have brought you here."

The air whooshed from his lungs as a concussive explosion slammed his back, forcing him to the ground.

Elizabeth Goddard is the award-winning author of more than thirty novels and novellas. A 2011 Carol Award winner, she was a double finalist in the 2016 Daphne du Maurier Award for Excellence in Mystery/Suspense, and a 2016 Carol Award finalist. Elizabeth graduated with a computer science degree and worked in high-level software sales before retiring to write full-time.

Visit the Author Profile page at Harlequin.com.

THREAD OF REVENGE

ELIZABETH GODDARD

HARLEQUIN® LOVE INSPIRED® SUSPENSE

Recycling programs
for this product may
not exist in your area.

LOVE INSPIRED BOOKS

ISBN-13: 978-1-335-54355-4

Thread of Revenge

www.Harlequin.com

Printed in U.S.A.

Be strong and of a good courage, fear not,
nor be afraid of them: for the Lord thy God, he it is that
doth go with thee; he will not fail thee, nor forsake thee.
                              –Deuteronomy 31:6

To Dan, my hero.

Acknowledgments

A writer can't create a novel in a vacuum. We can't write the stories alone. We need experts to help us get it right. Many thanks to those who helped me with various aspects of this story. Susan Sleeman—thanks for your police-procedural expertise and your brainstorming help. Martin Roy Hill—I couldn't have written this story without your expertise on all things Coast Guard. I especially appreciate your naming of the USCGC *Kraken*! And last but never least, I want to thank my editor, Elizabeth Mazer, and my agent, Steve Laube, for believing in my stories!

ONE

Her head throbbed and grogginess gripped her. She rocked as if on giant waves. A deep, aching chill touched her feet. The coldness licked at her toes until she slowly realized the sensation felt more than cold—it felt wet.

Salty water.

Giant, rolling waves.

Blinking, Sadie Strand pushed through the debilitating fuzziness and stirred completely awake. She drew in a breath. A small silver dolphin pendant pressed into the gray marine carpet near her cheek. Confusion racked her thoughts. She released the pendant from its snare and pushed up on her elbows, nausea washing over her again. *What? Where am I?* By the listing of her quarters, she realized she was on a boat and waves caused the swaying motion, the violent rocking. *Oh, no!*

She glanced down to her feet.

Water flooded the vessel.

Panic swept over her with the force of a tidal wave. And then the boat pitched with the next wave and cold water rushed over her. She gasped and choked until she caught her breath again.

What is going on? She didn't know how she'd ended up on this boat, but that didn't matter so much as how she was going to get off. She rolled to her knees to stand and get her sea legs to walk with the lurching, rolling of a boat in a storm. A sinking boat, no less.

Sadie made her way to the helm in search of the radio, aware that with each second that passed, the boat took on more water. Maybe she only needed to find the pump and expel the water from the storm, except it was already too late. The pump, if there was one, would be beneath the water that clearly rushed in from not only belowdecks, but above as waves crashed over the sinking vessel.

A drowning death was her worst nightmare. *Oh, God, please help me!* But it looked like that was exactly what was about to happen. Sadie was going to die in a watery grave.

Just like Karon.

That is, if she didn't find a way to survive, or if someone didn't come to her aid. At the helm, she found the radio and turned to the channel the Coast Guard, marine patrol or any other authorities might monitor.

"Mayday, Mayday, Mayday! I'm sinking. Is anyone out there? Mayday. Mayday!" Sadie repeated her calls. She glanced at the dash to relay her coordinates but nothing worked so she couldn't know her exact location. The cold water assured her she must be somewhere in the North Pacific off the Washington coast where she'd been before waking up on the boat.

How could this happen? She continued calling for help, then realization slowly dawned. In her panic she hadn't noticed the red light wasn't flickering. There wasn't the telltale squawk. Nothing. It was dead. The radio was unresponsive. Broken. Just like everything else.

That news hit her like an anchor, heavy and bone jarring. Someone had obviously sabotaged the vessel. They'd deliberately set her up to die.

Tears burned her eyes. "Oh, Karon," she whispered. "I wanted to know what happened… I wanted to know, and now I think I do. But I don't know why someone killed you. Or who!"

Memories rushed back at her. She'd been going through Karon's things, looking for a clue as to why her best friend's body had washed up on the beach. Then Sadie had woken up here. She had the sense that someone had been there in the house with her, but the image, the memory, was too vague. She couldn't be sure. Nor could she worry about that now. Her life was in imminent jeopardy. How could she find Karon's killer if she died too? And that gave her even more incentive to live. To survive. She had to find out who was behind this. She wouldn't let them get away with it.

She searched for a life jacket or flotation device or smaller skiff attached to this boat before it plunged, submerging completely. Anything to which she could cling that would keep her above the surface of a blustering North Pacific Ocean.

But her search left her empty-handed. "Nothing!" *Are you kidding me?*

Of course, why would she expect there to be a flotation device if the radio had been sabotaged?

Her teeth chattered. Even if she found something to help her float, hypothermia would soon set in. And panic—the absolute worst thing she could do right now—washed over her again, flooding her soul with terror.

What do I do? What do I do?

"Okay, so I'm not going to save this boat, but I can hang on until the very last minute in case someone comes to help." She said the words out loud, hoping to boost her confidence. But she fought against the reality of her dire predicament.

This wasn't a princess story with a knight in

shining armor to come to her rescue and guarantee a happy ending. And even if it were, she'd prefer to save herself.

Sadie went outside onto the deck to face the raging storm, and maybe even to face God. She stared up into the daunting black clouds as rain lashed her. "Why, God? Why?"

She felt so cliché in that moment, as if there had never been another person or literary character to stand in the rain to face the Creator of the universe—the calmer of storms, even—and ask that question. She searched for the horizon, but it was lost somewhere between the ocean and sky, both dark shades of gray.

How far was she from shore?

Could she swim?

In this weather, even if she didn't exhaust herself fighting the storm as she swam and actually made it to the coastline, the ocean waves could dash her against the rocks. Same with the boat if it had power so she could run the engine and steer it toward shore.

Okay. No radio. No flotation device. And in a few minutes—less than half an hour or less, she'd say—no boat. Someone had gone to a lot of trouble to kill her in a way that would look like an accident and there wouldn't be much evidence left behind to say otherwise. She was staying in Coldwater Bay with her aunt—a boating and fishing community. Boating accidents happened. But there would be no one to question her death like she questioned Karon's.

Why had someone killed her friend? Why were they trying to kill *her*? Some secret that was too important to expose?

The killer had to have made a mistake along the way. Sadie would be the one to find it. She wasn't about to give up. Except she hung on to the boat in water up to her chest. Frosty, biting water, and her limbs grew numb. Giving up might not be within her control.

Her teeth chattered as she tried to force out the words. "I'm sorry, Aunt Debby." And to her siblings, "Cora, Quinn and Jonna. I'm really sorry."

With their parents' tragic deaths more than a decade ago, they'd already lost so much, and losing Sadie would be so hard for them. Her death in this watery grave would leave them with questions instead of closure. She'd never felt so heartsick than in this moment when she realized there was nothing she could do—no grand scheme to win the day. No brilliant ideas that would save her from inescapable drowning.

Soaked and chilled to the bone despite his protective garb, CGIS—Coast Guard Investigative Service—special agent Gage Sessions stood at the helm of the *USCGC Kraken* with Lieutenant Johns, who had steered the eighty-seven-foot cutter straight into the storm. The twenty-foot swells had only just begun subsiding along with the fifty-knot winds as the storm slowly passed over them.

He'd joined the *Kraken*'s crew as part of a counter-drug smuggling operation, but one particular group eluded him. In the Pacific Northwest, the drug cartels were usually Russian or Asian. The last few months, intel had him chasing the Chang brothers, and he was getting close, but they always evaded him. He might have to work undercover if he was ever going to catch the brothers in the act.

In the interim, they'd received a distress call. Someone spotted a sinking boat and had shared the coordinates but were unable to assist.

Their counter-drug-smuggling operation had suddenly changed to a rescue mission.

Finding the sinking boat in the Pacific during a storm—well, it could already be too late. The boat had likely been tossed miles from the original location where it had been spotted. And in this storm, he didn't hold out much hope. But he wouldn't give up yet either.

God, please guide us. Show us where to find the boat, or PIW—person in water, as it might turn out. In that case, the PIW hopefully had on a life jacket or clung to a flotation device. That person would be hoping and praying that the Coast Guard would find and save them. Every minute, every second, counted.

If they had already lost the boat, they would be more easily missed. The vastness of the ocean was cruel in that way.

He was grateful they had been out here, as it was, on the eighty-seven-footer WPB-class Coast Guard patrol cutter—equipped to handle rescues on the high seas. Except, regardless of the equipment, there weren't enough Coast Guard vessels to adequately protect the ninety-five thousand miles of coastline. That was roughly four and a half million square miles of United States maritime territory. And that made Gage even more concerned they wouldn't find the sinking boat in time to rescue the person or people involved.

"I see something," Johns said.

His pulse jumped.

Gage caught sight of something in the water too, just before it disappeared behind another swell. Rain and waves beat the cutter and the small crew of the *Kraken*. Unlike the Chang brothers, who eluded them because of the storm, whoever was on that sinking boat out there was at the storm's mercy.

Gage gripped the rail, willing the *Kraken* to

fight the waves, to move faster as it clashed with the treacherous Pacific.

"Come on. If we lose sight of the object in the water now, we probably won't get another chance," Gage yelled over the spray of salt water that came with each gust.

He thought his words might have been lost to the wind even though he stood right next to the guy.

"You're not a crew member, Sessions," Johns shouted. "You could go back down where it's warm and dry and let us deal with it."

"There." Gage spotted the boat and his stomach plummeted with the crest of the wave. He could see only the top of the vessel. It was about to go under and someone held on to the bow. "Hurry or we'll be too late!"

Johns urged the *Kraken* closer.

"Throw the line, we'll drag him in!" Baines called.

Throw, row and go. That was the usual CG adage to rescue a sinking boat or someone who was about to drown.

A crew member tossed the line over the side, but the rough seas wouldn't cooperate. The boat dipped completely under.

"Throw it again."

Gage peered through binoculars, a challenge

with the high seas and constant rain. He caught a glimpse of someone...a woman.

He knew her.

Gage's heart squeezed.

No. It couldn't be. He swiped an arm over his eyes and blinked the rain and ocean away, frustrated with the wrath of nature. He trained his binoculars again. *Where are you? Where are you...*

There. In an instant, he got a good, close look at the panic-stricken face. The relief that the Coast Guard had arrived and the hope they would rescue her. The fact that he knew this woman sunk into his marrow.

That changed everything.

"Captain, we can't get the line to her. The storm is making that impossible."

"Let's take the inflatable out to her then." While crew members prepared the boat, Gage watched the swells overwhelm her. She appeared so small by comparison.

His gut tensed. "She's not going to make it if we don't get someone in the water now!"

"Get belowdecks now, Agent Sessions," Johns said. "This isn't part of your operation."

"I know that woman!" *I cared about her once.* And he still did.

Johns nodded to crew members behind Gage and they grabbed his arms, presumably to escort him belowdecks. Gage shrugged free. He lifted his hands in mock surrender. "I'm going, I'm going."

I'm going in to get her myself.

This time, Gage wasn't willing to wait around for them to cross every *t* and dot every *i*. For them to follow their rules and processes. Images of a failed rescue attempt during a storm like this accosted him.

And this was Sadie. He'd rather risk his life than sit by and watch this unfold before him. Gage prepared his own tender line and hooked himself up. He could act now and ask forgiveness later. The smaller boat wasn't even in the water yet. The tension in his gut twisted into a tight knot.

It was taking them far too long. The woman had minutes. Seconds even.

His actions were against all procedure.

"Hey, what are you doing?" someone shouted.

Uh-oh. Time was up. It was now or never.

The thick-necked Baines came running toward him, his intention to tackle Gage more than clear. He turned to confront the sea. A wave engulfed him as he stood ready to face off with the beast. Gage snatched a rescue buoy and dragged in a long, deep breath, then he launched himself into the shockingly cold water of the

Pacific. He would trust Baines to handle the tender line appropriately.

Gage was in the water, and he was going after the woman. End of discussion.

Shouts and whistles from the shocked crew joined the roar of the storm. He swam furiously against the invincible force of nature, the huge swells and rough water preventing him from catching his breath. Time wasn't on his side, but he swam forward with only one goal in mind.

Find her. Save her.

With Baines managing the tender line, Gage trusted he wouldn't be lost at sea, and kicked harder, fighting against this monster ocean railing in the storm. How much more difficult this would be if they weren't on the waning side of it.

Sadie was definitely the PIW—he saw her clearly now—and she waved at him, then dropped out of sight beneath the surface. In that glimpse of her, he realized she wore no life jacket. Treading water, she fought the sea on her own strength, which must be weakening. With his effort to reach her, his heart banged against his rib cage. Coast Guard protocol would dictate his objective was to establish communication with her, encourage and instruct her. Right. No time for that.

Please, God, let me save her!

Gage swam to where he last saw her. She hadn't resurfaced. She could be anywhere beneath the water. A current could have swept her far away from him.

"No!" He dove beneath the surface but the too-violent, dark water offered zero visibility.

The crew members of the *Kraken* shouted at him. Blew their whistles. He glanced back and saw them pointing. They must have spotted Sadie. They'd released the smaller boat into the water, as well. Good. Gage started swimming in the direction they pointed. He couldn't see her, but hoped he would connect.

Then she bobbed above the water, riding high on a rising swell. Gage had to get to her—he could see in her eyes that if he didn't reach her this time, she was done. Her lips were blue already. She had to be a good swimmer to have survived this long, but even his limbs would begin to fail him soon. He was pushing the limits.

Gage forced himself to swim harder and faster against one of the strongest forces of nature, and likewise Sadie swam toward him, her strength fading, her desperation warring against her biology. The swell crested and buried her again, sucking her down and under.

Gage dove beneath it, a calculated risk on his part, and gave one last thrusting lunge

He felt the tug of his tender line—the *Kraken* crew members trying to tow him back to safety.

"No, no!" He yanked the line, hoping someone would get his message, give him the slack he needed.

He tried again…

And touched something. A hand? He grabbed it, lunged forward and wrapped his arms around her body as he held on to the rescue buoy. Rescuing a drowning person was a dangerous task—that person was reduced to their basest survival instincts and would often drown their rescuers in the process.

Sadie had already turned into that drowning person.

And she fought him. Dragged him under. Instinctually. Nothing she could control. Her survival instincts had taken over. The right thing to do, and what protocol demanded, was that he hit her hard enough to knock her out and save them both. But since when had he gone with protocol? He grabbed her arms and willed her to be still, to trust him, and she relaxed.

Now. It was now or they would both be lost.

He felt the tug of his tender line, and he held on to her. His pulse shot up even higher, if that were possible. They breached the surface. When he looked in her face he saw why she'd

A marine archaeologist, Sadie's sister Cora explored shipwrecks. Admittedly, that made Sadie envious at times. And her DEA agent brother Quinn... Aunt Debby didn't even mention him. Nobody had heard from him in far too long. He preferred it that way.

Regardless, Sadie definitely didn't want her siblings involved because that could put them in danger, as well.

Though she hated causing her aunt more distress, the woman needed to know.

"Someone tried to kill me," she said.

Concern rippled over Aunt Debby's features and she slowly sat on the bed. "Why didn't you tell me this before?"

"Because I didn't want you to worry." Not yet. Not until she spoke again with Gage Sessions. She still struggled to grasp he'd been the one to rescue her. Save her life.

On the Coast Guard cutter that brought her to safety and the Coldwater Bay Hospital, Gage had been more than reassuring when he'd wrapped the blanket around her. Then at the hospital, he'd suggested she rest. She might remember more about what happened so she could answer the questions when someone came to investigate.

Sadie had last seen Gage in college over seven years ago. They'd been close friends then. He'd cared about her as more than a friend, she'd known, but she hadn't felt the same because she had been in love with someone else. Would the outcome have been different today if it had been a stranger rather than Gage risking his life to save hers?

Aunt Debby pressed her hand on Sadie's forehead as though checking her temperature, unease still evident in her eyes. "And you've told the sheriff?"

"I told the Coast Guard and someone is letting the sheriff's department know for me."

"Good. You've been through a lot. Just get some rest and once your core temperature is back up, they'll release you. I'll take you home and take care of you. Remember, you're not in this alone, Sadie."

"I know." And Sadie thanked God for her family.

She closed her eyes and rested on the pillow. She wished she could remember everything that had happened. One minute she was at Karon's house. The next she was on that boat fighting to survive. Who did the boat belong to, anyway? With it hidden in the depths of the Pacific, would she ever find out?

If only she could remember more. Was hypothermia messing with her memories? When she'd woken up on the boat, she'd been extremely groggy with the world's worst headache. That hadn't been hypothermia. No—she'd been drugged.

A flash of a memory zinged back to her.

Sadie glanced down at her hospital gown. "Aunt Debby?"

"Yes, sweetie?"

"Where are my clothes?"

Her aunt chuckled. "It's customary to wear a hospital gown in the hospital. Don't you remember changing?"

Vaguely. "No, I mean, what happened to them after I changed into this?"

"Oh, I took them home to wash and dry them."

Oh, no. "Could you do me a favor? I need you to go through the pockets of my hoodie. I found something on the boat. It could be important." The pendant was a link, the proof she needed that Karon had been on that same boat. Possibly evidence that Karon's killer was now after Sadie.

A chill crawled over her that had nothing to do with her recovery from hypothermia.

Aunt Debby agreed to search her pockets back at the house and left Sadie alone with her thoughts, which turned out to be a bad idea. She couldn't exactly rest like everyone insisted when someone had gone to such trouble to attempt to kill her.

She wished Jonna was here already. Her sister had been an ICE agent while living in Miami. Sadie didn't know what had happened in Florida to send Jonna running back to Washington. She only knew it had been something bad, and Jonna hadn't wanted to talk about it. So maybe she wouldn't help Sadie feel all that safe.

Fortunately, she didn't have long to fret. In walked Gage Sessions, his presence filling her with relief and the overwhelming impression that she was safe with him. And why shouldn't it? He'd saved her today, after all, and she could still sense the protectiveness, the heroism, pouring off him. But she didn't want him to notice just how relieved she was to see him. More to the point…

"Gage, I remember." She sat up in bed. "It's starting to come back to me now."

"You mean why you were on the boat?"

"Well, sort of. That part is still fuzzy, but what happened before."

He moved closer to the bed, his form trim and fit, his jaw strong and his bright hazel eyes sharp. With his sun-bleached hair, he was the same guy from a few years ago, yes, but there was something different about him. He seemed more self-assured. Experienced. A thrill ran through her. *Really, Sadie. Focus.*

"Well, I'm listening." He crossed his arms and leaned against the wall closest to her bed.

"Okay, give me a second." She squeezed her eyes shut and dragged in a few breaths. "I'd gone to Karon's house with her mother's approval. Her mother had thought Karon's death suspicious and I agreed. It's hard to believe that Karon, a marine science major working at an environmental company, a good swimmer and certified scuba diver, had drowned. If she'd intended to swim at all for some sort of research, she would have at least had on a dry suit to keep her warm. Karon had taken time off and was staying at their vacation rental house on the coast. Her mother—who lived on the other side of Coldwater Bay in Joshua—was planning to meet her there when she could get off work. Karon never returned to the house but instead her body was found…" Sadie couldn't even choke out the rest. She closed her eyes and tried to shove aside the deep anguish in her heart at the loss of her very dearest friend.

When she opened her eyes again and looked at Gage, his gaze was penetrating. Almost accusing. "So you went to her house for your own investigation."

She shrugged. "Yeah. There wasn't any crime scene tape or anything. The authorities ruled her drowning death an accident."

"What happened next?"

She tried to picture everything in her mind. Tried to remember it all. "Her vacation rental house is right along the beach above the rocks. I remember thinking how apropos that the storm clouds were brewing in the distance. I couldn't understand why no one in law enforcement found her death suspicious."

"They'll listen now, Sadie, since someone tried to kill you."

She was glad she could talk to him and he really listened and believed her. It was just like old times, only much more serious. "Not just someone, Gage. The same person."

"Keep talking."

"I came back for the funeral. I'd been in Indonesia researching for a grant I desperately need—I'm a marine biologist now—when I got the call. Nothing could have brought me back. Nothing except the death of someone I love. Do you understand?"

His expression turned somber yet compassionate. He moved closer, appearing absorbed in her story. "Yes, I think I do. What happened next at Karon's house? I want to know how you ended up on the boat."

He questioned her like an investigator, keeping her on track. "Well, I remember something crashed outside the house. I thought it was a garbage can. I glanced out the window but saw nothing but branches scratching the glass with the gust of wind. I booted up Karon's laptop and what I found stunned me. I guess it shouldn't have."

Gage inched closer. "What did you find?"

"The thing had been wiped clean."

"And did you call the authorities?"

"No. That's where my memories grow fuzzy and unclear. I had this creepy sensation that someone was watching me. I can't say for sure but I think someone was there with me. I remember…someone. Just not who or even what they looked like. If it was a man or a woman. And the next thing I remember is waking up on that sinking boat with no radio or flotation devices. My head was pounding, and I felt woozy, weird, like the effects of a drug wearing off. Someone wanted me dead. Talk about the perfect crime."

When she lifted her gaze to meet Gage's, he appeared visibly shaken. "It would only have been the perfect crime if you had died. Sounds like you were definitely drugged. But did the person responsible intend for the drugs to keep you asleep until you drowned? Or had they meant for you to wake up and know the situation was hopeless, which could mean a personal motive for murder? Either way..." Gage cleared his throat instead of finishing the sentence.

His deep concern surprised her.

She would finish the sentence for him. "Either way, it means I'm still in danger once they know I survived."

Gage paced the hallway outside Sadie's hospital room. He hadn't revealed his role as an investigator for the Coast Guard because he didn't want to give her false hope that he would help her. Or that his SAC—special agent in charge—would assign him. Another CGIS special agent, Thompkins, had already investigated Karon's death along with the sheriff's office and ruled it an accident.

Could they have been wrong? That's why Gage had wanted to question Sadie himself. That, and, well...they'd been friends. In that sense he would always be there for her, and it seemed that life had a torturous way of bringing them back together every few years.

He had no other responsibility to her and could have gone straight back to work, but for two things.

Her words to him about someone trying to kill her.

And the fact that it was Sadie Strand that he'd pulled from the ocean. He couldn't believe it when he finally realized who the woman in the water was. He couldn't believe it when he'd swum to her, fighting against the ferocious Pacific, and finally gathered her into his arms. He wasn't someone easily traumatized.

But that incident had shaken him.

They'd grown up in the same small town in Coldwater Bay. Had gone to school together. He'd had a crush on her back then, but she'd never noticed him. Then they'd met again at the University of Washington in Seattle and had become close friends. Frequently shared long walks on the beach. And yeah, he'd gotten that crush on her again.

She hadn't noticed that time either because she'd been smitten with someone else. At least that's what he told himself. Maybe it had been a lie. Regardless, there was always someone else to catch her attention. Of course, that had been years before and Gage had gotten over her a long time ago. They'd been friends and he would always care about her that way. None of those residual romantic feelings remained, for which he was grateful. Still, finding her and saving her from near death had unsettled him.

He waited in the hall now for someone from the sheriff's department so he could share what she'd told him and watch his reaction. A deputy sheriff strode straight for Gage. He knew the investigative deputy, Bob Crowley, and tried to work with him when their investigations crossed, but that wasn't always possible.

"Good to see you, Sessions," Deputy Crowley said. "Sorry it took me so long to get here."

"Not a problem." It gave him an excuse to hang around and talk himself out of going back into Sadie's room.

"Tell me what you know." Looking beat, Crowley rubbed his neck as if he'd already pulled an all-nighter.

Gage told him what Sadie had shared with him, including her belief that Karon was murdered and she'd become the target now. "I asked the doctor to run blood tests to find out what drug is in Sadie's system."

"Karon Casings's death was already ruled an accident. That comes from me. The other CGIS agent looked into it since she was Coast Guard reserve and decided her death had nothing to do with her duties, so he didn't have any jurisdiction. Maybe Sadie is distraught over her death and not thinking clearly. Her story sounds farfetched," Crowley added. "What do you think?"

Was Crowley serious? Or was Gage's relationship with Sadie clouding his judgment about the facts? He didn't think so. He believed someone had tried to kill her, but he based that solely on her word. Gage hesitated with a reply. He didn't want to give too much away. He believed it was always best to wait and watch people. "I guess it all depends on why someone would want to kill Karon, and then Sadie? Any ideas on that?"

"None." Crowley frowned and glanced up and down the hallway.

Gage would talk to Agent Thompkins about it too. Two investigators claimed Karon's death was an accident. What had they missed? Was it possible that Karon's death had, in fact, been an accident, but someone had tried to kill Sadie and they were two separate cases? Sadie had been in Karon's home when she'd been abducted and placed on the boat to die. No. Definitely connected.

Gage pressed his fist against his lips and thought about Sadie. She'd been all about protecting marine life and conservation. All about justice for those who couldn't protect themselves. Gage didn't feel comfortable walking away from this, walking away from her. And if this was connected to Karon and her death hadn't been an accident—what was going on? Could he let someone else investigate even if he had no jurisdiction?

No. No, he couldn't. In the end, his SAC would have the last say, but Gage could be persuasive when he wanted. He just needed a valid motive.

Then finally, he said, "We'll see what the blood test says. I'll talk to my SAC. We might need to reopen Karon Casings's investigation too."

Crowley pursed his lips, hung his head and shook it. "I thought you were in the middle of trying to catch the drug smugglers off our coast. What are you even doing here, Sessions?"

"I pulled Sadie from the water. Or did I forget to mention that? But you're right. I'm working on drug runners." He'd just have to handle both cases. "So what's it going to be, Crowley? Are you going to listen to her story or not?"

"All right. I'll go talk to her." Crowley put his hands on his hips. "But Karon's death was an accident. End of story. Maybe I can convince her of that."

Maybe, but you can't convince me just yet after what happened today. Gage held his tongue and nodded, still troubled by everything that had happened and unsure what he was supposed to do. Uncertain if he could leave Sadie to face this with anyone except him by her side. With Crowley to look into things. It would all depend on his SAC's take on it. But what if the man didn't want to reopen the Casings investigation? What about Sadie? Someone had tried to kill her and she wasn't Coast Guard. Crowley would be in charge of that. Could he trust the deputy to protect her and find the truth?

Gage's cell rang. He glanced at the phone. Crowley waited for him to take the call, acting as if he had more to say. Gage answered.

"I've got some news." It was his SAC—Jim Sullivan—at the regional headquarters in Seattle.

"What's happened?"

"Lieutenant Sean Miller's body washed up. Two bullets to the back. The same kind of bullets your drug runners use. So it could definitely be tied to your investigation, Gage. I need you to get to the scene the next county up." Jim relayed the coordinates and ended the call. Well, that was it then. His spirits sank at the thought of leaving Sadie, but he had his orders. He'd talk to Jim about what happened today, but Gage doubted he would see Sadie any time soon until fate pushed them together again.

He lifted his gaze to meet Crowley's. "A Coastie's body washed up on the beach north of Coldwater Bay. Next county over, so your counterpart will meet me there to conduct his own investigation. I guess I have my marching orders. I'll leave you to take care of Sadie." And saying those words pained him more than it should. She wasn't his responsibility. He struggled to force one foot in front of the other to leave her and trudged slowly toward the exit.

"Sessions, wait."

Gage slowed and turned around. "What?"

"That would be the second body in two weeks, wouldn't it? The other one belonged to Karon Casings, as you know. But Karon's mother told me that Karon had been seeing someone. He'd been on leave and nobody could tell me where he'd gone. But he didn't come to her funeral."

Gage stiffened. Could it be? "What was his name?"

Crowley's lips flattened. "Lieutenant Sean Miller."

Gage glanced at the door to Sadie's hospital room. And Karon Casings had been Sadie Strand's best friend. The three incidents were all connected.

Fear fisted around his heart and wouldn't let go. Sadie was in danger.

THREE

Exhaustion would overwhelm her soon. She hoped the deputy would finish up.

"Thanks for answering my questions," Deputy Crowley said. "You're sticking around town in case we have more, right?"

"Of course. I'm not leaving until I know who's responsible for what happened to Karon. Finding out who tried to kill me today will give me that answer."

Deputy Crowley angled his head, a deep crease in his brow. "We'll see what we can find out. I need a number and an address where I can reach you if I have further questions."

"I live with my aunt Debby." She gave him the address.

After college she'd been busy traveling, working and researching and never actually took the time to move out. But someone had attempted to kill her; she should reconsider staying at the house.

"We know where to find you then. Get some rest." He turned to leave and just as he reached the door, she called out.

He turned to face her. "Yes, ma'am?"

"The other man, the one who pulled me out of the water."

"Special Agent Sessions?"

Special agent? Why hadn't she known he was in law enforcement, a special agent, at that? She'd assumed he was Coast Guard. He'd been on the Coast Guard cutter. She frowned. "Gage Sessions. Is he still out in the hallway?"

He shook his head. "No, ma'am. He left a while ago."

She sagged at the news, surprised at how disappointed she was.

"Can I do anything for you?" he asked.

"Do you know if he's coming back?"

"I couldn't say, but it all depends on if he's involved with the investigation."

She nodded and the deputy exited.

After the hospital staff had come in to get her signature on release papers, she waited on Aunt Debby to give her a ride home.

Sadie rubbed her head, which still felt a little woozy. And after she got home, then what? She weighed her options. Common sense told her to go back to her research on the other side of the world and let the authorities find out who tried to kill her—she'd be safer that way too. Let them find out who had murdered Karon. But as a marine biologist, she was also a researcher—she conducted scientific investigations, as it were. She didn't trust anyone else to be as thorough as she would be. Conducting her own investigation would mean putting her future on hold indefinitely—possibly missing her chance at the grant she wanted. Still, there was nothing more important to her than bringing Karon's murderer to justice. And she wasn't entirely confident that Deputy Crowley was the man for the job.

She hoped that Gage would be involved. But she was getting ahead of herself. First she needed to get out of this hospital room.

Someone knocked lightly on the door. "Sadie?"

Gage's voice rang out. The sound warmed her.

"Come in."

He opened the door and stepped all the way into the room. His shoulders were broad. And his arms. She remembered those strong arms around her, scooping her against him as she nearly drowned, swimming her to the smaller boat that took them to the Coast Guard cutter. The *Kraken*, if she remembered correctly.

An image came to mind. Gage Sessions

swooping down from the *Kraken* to rescue her. And she'd thought it wasn't a princess story, and more than that, she'd wanted to save herself. Ha!

She realized she was grinning.

He studied her with those alert hazel eyes, which seemed to take in every detail, everything about her. Her cheeks warmed. She was glad he couldn't read her mind.

"It's good to see you have your color back." His smile was engaging.

"I'm so glad to see you. I wasn't sure if you were coming back."

His expression turned serious. "Of course. I had to make sure you're going to be okay."

"Earlier when you were here, I forgot to thank you for pulling me from the ocean."

"You're welcome."

"I hope they didn't give you a hard time. I heard that you kind of broke protocol." And she wondered why. She had a feeling his willingness to risk his life in the ocean for her, and willingness to go against the Coast Guard's protocol, had saved her life.

"Anything for a friend." He jammed his hands in his pockets. "So…how are you doing? Really?"

She leaned back in the chair. That was a good question. Sadie closed her eyes to think. Looking at Gage was too distracting. She didn't remember that about him from before. "I'm still shaky after everything."

"That's understandable." Gage sat on the edge of the bed.

She opened her eyes. Yeah, he was still a distraction. "So what happens next?"

"Someone will investigate on your behalf, Sadie, don't worry. In the meantime, my office will be looking into the death of your friend Karon again. We've learned some new information that gives us reason to believe you could be right that she was murdered."

Sadie released a heavy sigh. "New information…you mean something more than I told you about what happened to me?"

He nodded gravely, but didn't look like he was going to reveal anything else.

"Gage, you said your office. You mean the Coast Guard? You were on that cutter. What exactly do you do in the Coast Guard? The deputy called you a special agent. And you're investigating. You never told me anything. I figured you'd just jumped in the water for me because you were part of the Coast Guard cutter."

"I'm CGIS. Coast Guard Investigative Services. But I'm a civilian, not military. CGIS is a federal law enforcement agency. We operate outside the Coast Guard chain of command. That said, some agents are active duty military and others are Coast Guard reserve. And others like me are civilian special agents."

"Oh." Well, now, that was something. Impressive.

"And… I jumped in the water when I saw it was you. I had to save a friend." That grin again.

What would have happened to her if she hadn't had a friend out there today? Still, Karon hadn't had a friend when she'd needed one. Fatigue tugged at Sadie and she yawned. "I want to help you with your investigation into Karon's murder."

"Wait. One, I'm not sure I'll be the one to investigate. Two, you aren't helping with the investigation, regardless. Let the authorities do their job without your interference. You don't want to stand in the way of the process or hinder the investigation…or mess with evidence. Besides, it could be dangerous. Don't forget, someone tried to kill you today." He hung his head as if that thought disturbed him deeply, then raised it again.

"I haven't forgotten, believe me. It's obviously related, don't you see?" Her voice pitched higher than usual, and a little too loud for the close quarters.

"Yes, I see. I assure you we'll get to the bottom of this."

"Gage, please see if they will let you be the one to investigate."

"I don't know. I'm already involved in another case—that's how I ran into you on the ocean. I was out chasing down drug runners when we learned about your sinking boat."

"I'd feel so much better if it were you—someone I know and trust. Will you talk to your boss?"

His forehead wrinkled.

"I mean, unless you don't feel comfortable. I'm sorry. I guess I overstepped."

"It's not that." He leveled his intense gaze on her again. "I'm concerned for your safety."

And her heart swelled. She had the feeling if the deputy had told her the same thing, it wouldn't have meant nearly as much.

"I'm back, sweetie." Aunt Debby entered the room carrying a plastic bag of toiletries and clothes.

Aunt Debby nodded. "Hey, Gage. Good to see you again."

He smiled. "Same here."

Sadie grabbed the toiletries and clothes and changed in the bathroom.

When she stepped out fully dressed, Aunt Debby looked her up and down. "Oh. They're releasing you so soon?"

Sadie chuckled. "You act like that's a bad thing."

"Well, no, it's not. As long as you're better and they're not rushing the process."

"I've been waiting on a wheelchair for half an hour. I wouldn't call that rushing."

"Why didn't you call me? I would have come right back and lit a fire under them."

"Now that you're here maybe you can alert the nurse so we can get out of here."

"I will. Just a second." Her aunt dug around in her pocket. "Oh, I found that item you were looking for."

She handed it to Sadie, then left the room. Sadie lifted the small dolphin pendant up to examine it in the light.

"What's that?" Gage asked.

"Proof that Karon was on that same boat that sank today."

Gage stiffened. This could be an important piece of evidence.

She held the silver pendant out. "It's a dolphin. I gave it to her on her twenty-first birthday."

Scraping a hand through his hair, he paced the room. The nurse pushed a wheelchair through the door, Aunt Debby behind her.

"All right. Your aunt tells me you're ready to go home," the nurse said.

Sadie nodded.

Gage couldn't walk away from this. He'd been to the beach, met with the coroner and watched as Sean's body was removed. Sean's death had likely occurred two weeks after Karon's, but that didn't mean they weren't related. And it was tied to the attempt on Sadie's life somehow. His drug running investigation would normally take second place to a Coast Guard murder investigation, but his SAC wanted to know if the deaths were somehow tied to the drug runners. He could still assign Thompkins and not Gage. Since Gage had absolutely no intention of leaving Sadie without protection, he'd give Jim another call to press him.

And if Jim gave him what he wanted—to work the investigation on Sadie's attempted murder as it tied to Karon's death, which would give him the opportunity to protect her, Gage had to be careful. Under no circumstances could he let himself crush on her again.

An image flitted through his mind of them walking the beach together years ago. He'd been enamored with her, but all she talked about was the Coastie she was in love with. Gage had been able to get over her then. He'd moved on and found someone who returned his affection, and he allowed himself to fully, completely love. But that had left him heartbroken in the end.

Lesson learned—love wasn't for him.

And carrying that lesson in his back pocket, no way would he have a thing for Sadie this time, no matter how much time they spent together. But his protective instincts had kicked into full throttle. He had to stick close enough for long enough to protect her and help her find the truth. He'd make a call to his SAC and hope for the best.

All this he considered as he walked alongside Sadie as the nurse pushed her in the wheelchair down the hallway.

"Sadie. I have a question about the dolphin pendant," he said. "You woke up on a sinking boat and you thought to grab that?"

"My cheek was pressed into the carpet. The pendant was there when I opened my eyes. It was small but I recognized it, so I grabbed it."

Gage tugged a latex glove from his pocket and held his palm out as she handed it over.

"You think you're going to find prints on that after what it's been through?" Aunt Debby asked.

He eyed her. "Has it been through the wash?"

"Well, if you count the ocean…"

"You never know. Maybe the tiniest fiber could be important, and it's still there." He stuck it in one of the small evidence bags he kept in his pocket. The sheriff's department would take the lead on murder and attempted murder investigations, but the Coast Guard would conduct a parallel investigation of their own since a Coastie had been a victim, and they believed it could be tied to the drug runners. CGIS had jurisdiction over maritime drug smuggling. Gage hoped he could find the evidence he needed for jurisdiction. He would have to consider if he should turn this pendant over to Crowley or send it to be analyzed himself—that is, if he was assigned to the investigation. Otherwise, it would go to Thompkins.

"Wow, you're prepared, aren't you?"

"Always. In fact, I'm going to grab my vehicle and meet you at the exit." He took off down the hallway and headed out the door. He jogged over to his SUV, holding the dolphin, proof, Sadie claimed, that Karon had been on that boat. It could be something. It could be nothing.

Inside the vehicle, he called his SAC at the regional headquarters in Seattle as he maneuvered over to the hospital doors where Sadie and her aunt would soon exit.

"Jim, glad I caught you."

"You're just the man I was about to call."

"Oh?"

"Both CGIS special agent Thompkins and the

sheriff's department investigated Karon Cas-ings's death. You likely already know that noth-ing led them to conclude her death had been foul play or that the Coast Guard had any jurisdic-tion, even if it had been. I'm reopening the in-vestigation into Karon's death." Jim hesitated, then said, "Gage, I need fresh eyes on this. With what you've told me about Sadie Strand, if you dig into who put her on that boat to die, you might find a link to Karon's death and to your drug runners. You and Thompkins can work it from different angles."

"I agree, sir. It has to be related." Gage thought he heard something more in Jim's words—some emotion he couldn't quite pin down. Suspicion? "What if Karon and Sean had been on a boat? Maybe they ran into trouble out there. Sean was held against his will then shot and killed later so they washed up on shore at separate times." How did all of this play into Sadie's abduction and attempted murder?

"It's your job to figure it out. And Gage..."

"Yes, sir?"

"We need to wrap this up quickly. I don't want another Coastie washing up onto the beach." Anger infused Jim's tone, but Gage knew it wasn't directed at him.

He ended the call, pleased on the one hand that he could stay close to Sadie, keep an eye out, as he investigated. But there was a down-side to that—he'd have to stay close to Sadie.

When he pulled around the circular hospital drive for pickup and drop-off, Sadie was just being wheeled out the door, her aunt Debby plodding faithfully behind her. He hopped out and went around to open the door for her.

"What are you doing, Gage?" Debby asked. "I can take her home."

He assisted Sadie up into his SUV, soaking in her smile.

"But we're not going home, are we, Special Agent Sessions?" Her blue eyes shimmered with expectation.

And her smile engaged his heart a little too much so he looked back at her aunt. "Debby, if it's all right with you, Sadie and I have somewhere to go. But I'll take you over to your car so you don't have to walk."

"Nonsense. I can walk. I need the exercise. And for pity's sake, the girl just got out of the hospital." Her aunt appeared nonplussed, but her eyes twinkled as though she was glad something was going on between them. And Gage wished he hadn't noticed that. Because he wasn't taking Sadie out for a date. Nothing was going on between them.

"He's taking me over to Karon's vacation house, Aunt Debby." Sadie leaned out the door and kissed her aunt on the forehead. "Don't worry. I'll be home for dinner."

She was right about their destination, but what on earth had given her the idea he was taking her to Karon's vacation house? Did she really know him that well? Or was it just the next logical step in the investigation?

Her aunt shook her head and walked off, mumbling to herself, though she had a teasing tone. "Kids these days."

Gage climbed into the driver's side. After she settled into the passenger seat, Sadie tilted her head toward him.

"I didn't tell you I was assigned the investigation yet," he said. "It's awfully presumptuous for you to think I was, and then to include yourself in it, which isn't how I normally work." Still, he couldn't help but grin at her. "So how did you know?"

"What, that we're going back to the last place Karon had been? The last place I was before the boat?"

He nodded and shifted the SUV into gear. He'd follow Debby to her car and see that she got in and drove off. Then he'd call Crowley to let him know in case the man wanted to meet them there. He hoped they had already put crime scene tape up again since Sadie had been abducted from that location. Gage would officially be investigating Karon's murder. And yes, he'd refer to it as a homicide now even if Crowley objected.

Sadie glanced his way, and he felt the tug of her gaze. He idled in the parking lot while Aunt Debby climbed into her midsize sedan.

"Because I can show you what the other guys missed and you know that," Sadie said. "And I figure that you're a hero, Gage, and there's a killer still out there. That's a ticking time bomb waiting to go off and I'm at the center of that explosion once he learns I survived. Now what are you going to do about it?"

FOUR

A ticking time bomb. Man, she had a way with words—a way to put the situation into a whole new perspective as if it were only a matter of time before the killer got his hands on her again and would finish the job. Gage already believed she was in danger. Her words had a profound effect on him, causing fear to cinch his throat.

"What am I going to do about it? Glad you asked. I have every intention of finding the person responsible." *And of protecting you, while I'm at it, Sadie Strand.*

"So you're the one who is going to investigate?" Her tone held a measure of hope.

That shouldn't make him happy, but it did.

Sadie's aunt safely in her car, Gage steered his vehicle out of the hospital parking lot. "Yes. I talked to my SAC. I've been assigned to investigate. Though Karon's death was initially ruled an accident, there's been another incident in addition to your attempted murder." He'd alluded to it earlier but hadn't told Sadie about Sean yet.

"And what's that?"

"Listen, Sadie, let's make one thing clear. I'm taking you to where you were abducted so that it will possibly trigger your memory. Whatever you tell me will help me to find Karon's killer and your abductor all in one, but other than that, you're not investigating with me. Understand?"

"Oh, really? You need me, special agent man. I know things that can help you, like you just said. For instance, I brought up the wiped computer hard drive and we're going to check on that now and see if we can find anything else."

"We won't touch the computer if it's there. I'll have to call in a computer tech if we want anything found to be used in a criminal case. The fact that you already touched it could ruin that for us, but we'll take this one step at a time. For my part, I'm only interested in what we can find as it ties to Karon's duties as a Coast Guard reservist or to the maritime drug smuggling ring I'm investigating."

"I don't understand. Aren't you trying to find who killed her?"

Yes and no. How did he explain?

"I'm investigating her murder as it pertains to the ring. Finding whoever left you out there could lead me to those involved. Was Karon murdered by the drug runners? Those who are involved in the ring? Or was she involved with them somehow?"

"What? No way!"

"Those were just sample questions. Was she associated with anyone possibly connected to the drug runners and maritime smuggling ring?" Yes, with Sean, depending on how he tied into it. Thompkins was looking into that.

"I don't know of anyone."

"What else can I learn about her murder that will lead me to the smugglers who will either be arrested for her murder or for drug running, or both? That's why I will work with the sheriff's department and other law enforcement entities as necessary. My goal is to determine if charges can be brought under the laws the Coast Guard enforces."

Sadie appeared to slump as if disappointed. He touched her arm. "You should know something. If my SAC hadn't assigned me, I would have pushed for it." Now, why did he think she had needed to know that?

But her spirits appeared to lift, so he'd been right to share.

"Thank you, Gage. I'm glad you're the one to find Karon's killer. And… I feel safe when I'm with you." She averted her gaze as if it was too hard to see his reaction to her words.

They had served only to further ignite his protectiveness.

He needed to focus back on task. "I'll have to meet up with the other CGIS special agent and get his notes. I'll read them tonight. But the fact that you were abducted from Karon's house and left to drown on a sinking boat suggests there must be something in the house worth looking at."

"And someone doesn't want me digging around and finding out who killed Karon."

A lump grew in his throat. He'd saved Sadie from the ocean, from the attempted murder. He prayed to God he could protect her until they caught the killer. Karon's killer. Like his SAC had said, he wanted this solved quickly so no one else would die. Gage couldn't agree more.

On the lengthy drive from the hospital back to the coast, he contacted Deputy Crowley and left a message that they were headed to the Casingses' vacation house. A long peninsula separated Coldwater Bay from the ocean. Several rivers emptied into the bay bordered by a few small towns—Joshua, West Plymouth, Oyster City, Bay City and Jackson—where Sadie lived with her aunt on the cove side of Coldwater Bay. Finally, Gage steered the SUV down Ocean-view Drive on the Washington state coastline, nearing the rental house where Karon had been staying.

Before him, the rock-studded coastline slid by.

Sadie leaned her elbow against the door and rested her chin on her hand. "Everything seems so surreal."

Gage understood what she meant. Sadie had been out in the middle of stormy waters mere hours ago and had almost died. Likely would have if the *Kraken* hadn't been on those waters, and maybe even if Gage hadn't been there. Still, he wanted to keep her talking and asked, "How's that?"

"I was just thinking about Coldwater Bay. The history of this place. Decades ago. A century ago even, this place was busy with trafficking, smuggling, and other crimes. But now it's so peaceful as if none of that ever happened, with a thriving tourist economy. I guess after everything that happened today, I should say it only seems peaceful."

"It seems like a dream that I grew up here and am back in Coldwater Bay on an investigation." *With you, no less!* It hit too close to home. Fate was cruel or God had a sense of humor. He could decide which when this was over.

Finally, they neared Karon's vacation house.

Gage parked in the street in front, half on the grass, half on the asphalt. A sand drive led up to the house.

He shifted to face Sadie.

"It also seems like a dream that I almost drowned today. And that Karon is gone. Murdered." She angled her head.

He wished she wouldn't look at him like that, her soft blue eyes reminding him of moments like this in college. But several years and life experiences had changed them both. And today's incident had also likely changed Sadie in ways she didn't even realize yet.

She reached for the door handle. "She would never have been out in the water that cold without a dry suit."

"That's why things like that are called accidents, but now that it appears someone tried to stop you from interfering, we have to look deeper." And end this before someone else got killed.

She opened the door.

"Sadie, wait." Gage jumped out and ran around to stand in her way. "Wait for me. I've been put on this case now, sure, but it's more than that. You can show me things I might not otherwise notice, yes, but the initial investigators have already searched the house for clues. Though they didn't find anything, as you know, we should still be careful not to disturb anything that could turn out to be evidence or help us find out who did this to Karon." He might want to bring in forensics. Since neither Thompkins nor Crowley had thought Karon had been murdered, they had likely missed something.

"Don't you think I know that?" Her brows furrowed. "The initial investigators missed the proof. They probably didn't even look at her computer. But I did and found it wiped clean."

"Maybe they looked and found nothing suspicious. Maybe it wasn't wiped when they were there, or they had no reason to even look. I'll have to read through the report, like I said." He held out his hand. "Come on. Let's go."

The sudden sense that someone was watching them crawled over him. Trees butted up near the house, which faced the ocean. Waves crashed against the rocks behind them. He squeezed her hand. Was he making a mistake?

A door shut. A man in a red cap that shadowed his face exited the house.

Gage froze. The man spotted him and took off running into the thick temperate forest that hugged the Washington coast.

"Wait in the truck." Gage tossed the keys to Sadie and ran after the man.

"I'm not waiting here!" She followed Gage around the house and into the woods, but soon fell behind. He couldn't leave her there alone. He'd lost the man anyway.

Gage backtracked through the trees and found Sadie behind a tree. He grabbed her hand and kept walking back toward his SUV. "This is too dangerous. I should never have brought you here." He tugged his cell out to call for backup.

The air whooshed from his lungs as a concussive explosion slammed his back, forcing him to the ground.

Sadie lifted her face out of the sand, gasping for breath. What just happened? Her ears were ringing. Strong arms gripped her. Pulled her up and against a wide chest. Once again she found herself in Gage's capable arms.

His face appeared blurry. His mouth was moving, but she couldn't hear his words, understand them. But she knew he asked if she was okay.

She nodded. "I think…" How could she be sure? She focused on Gage. "Are you okay?"

He looked dazed himself. They sat there together for a few seconds.

Flames consumed the house—Karon's family vacation house. Gage stood and pulled Sadie to her feet.

Dizziness swept over her, but she ignored it

as she took in the utter devastation heating up the air around them. "Oh, no, Gage."

Though her ears were still ringing, she heard her own voice this time.

He searched the ground near their feet and closer to the SUV.

"What are you looking for?" Sadie noticed a few chunks of the house—the roof, shards of glass from the windows, a splintered door—all these unintentional deadly weapons littered the yard.

"My cell. I was about to call for backup. Now we need emergency services. A fire truck."

They could have been killed a thousand times over. They could have been inside the house when it blew up. *Thank You, God!* Her knees wanted to buckle but she refused to give in.

"There. I see it." Sadie pointed at his cell on the ground a few yards away. She stuck close to him as he found the phone and examined it.

His demeanor on edge, he made a call as he held her gaze. "It's ringing. Seems to be working fine."

Phone to his ear, he led Sadie back to his SUV and they both climbed in. He locked the doors as he relayed the information regarding the blast. When he ended the call, he reached for Sadie's hand, hesitated, then pulled back.

"They're sending an ambulance too. I want

you to go with them. You need to make sure you don't have a concussion or internal injuries."

"I think I'd know if I did." Wouldn't she? Though she couldn't say she'd ever experienced a concussion before, or internal injuries for that matter. "And what about you? You need to make sure you're all right too. Don't try to be all tough guy on me, CGIS special agent Gage Sessions."

She dragged out his name as an attempt to add humor to the situation, but it rolled over him. His gaze darkened. "I've been through worse. I need to stay and talk to the sheriff. He might be calling in state police at this point. Lots of law enforcement to deal with, and I need to stay connected."

"I understand, but I don't want to leave. I want to be part of it too."

"You're not an investigator, Sadie. I know you tried by looking through her house, but it's not safe for you here at the moment." He worked his jaw. "Whoever was in the house must have planted an explosive device. Or they could have cut the gas lines and rigged it to explode to possibly look like an accident."

"Except we saw him leaving. But I didn't get a good look."

"Unfortunately, neither did I, but I know it was a man. He wore a red cap. I know his height and approximate weight. And he could still be out there somewhere watching us from a distance." He reached over and this time he took her hand. "I won't lie to you. Investigating is turning out to be more dangerous than I thought, but I want to keep you close. I want to make sure you're okay and stay that way. I want to protect you if I can, but I'm not sure how I can do both."

Protect her? Sadie wasn't sure how to take his words. Was he saying them from his position as a CGIS special agent? Or was it coming from somewhere inside of him? Something far more personal. At the thought, her heart tingled with warmth that was more than what she should feel for a friend. She and Gage had been friends before and they were still friends. She trusted him with her life, but feeling something more for him? That would never work. Even though he wasn't active duty or reserve Coast Guard and instead worked for CGIS as a civilian, he might as well be a Coastie, and Sadie had written off falling for a Coastie ever again.

Another smaller explosion at the house rocked the SUV. Sadie jumped and let out a small yelp. Gage leaned closer to her and together they watched the house now completely destroyed as the bright, hot flames continued to devour it.

A shudder ran over her.

Sadie pressed her face in her hands and leaned forward. Sucked in a few breaths.

Gage's hand pressed against her back. "Sadie?"

"I'm good. I'm fine." Karon had been murdered. Sadie had almost been murdered. And now Karon's house. "I don't understand. Why would someone go to all this trouble?"

Sirens resounded in the distance, coming from Bay City to the south. She sat up and watched the volunteer fire truck that carried a huge tank of water lumber up the drive to the house. The sheriff's vehicles soon followed and parked along the street next to Gage's SUV, and then the ambulance.

"Here's your ride, Sadie."

She didn't want to go. She wouldn't argue with him, but would simply ask the EMTs to look her over and leave her behind. Then Gage would have to keep her close, and she could find out more.

He exited the SUV and she followed his lead, getting out before he had the chance to open the door for her. He guided her over to the ambulance and handed her off to the EMT that jumped out. "You'll be in safe hands now. I need to talk to the sheriff."

Gage disappeared up the drive.

The EMT's name was Gary and he assisted her onto a gurney, but she refused to lie down.

"I'm okay. You can give me a once-over, but I'm not going anywhere with you."

The scrawny, much-too-young-looking guy arched a brow. "If I find something that needs attention, you might change your mind."

"I just got out of the hospital earlier today. I'm not changing my mind. I don't want to go back for any reason."

Gary listened to her heart and checked her vitals. Looked in her eyes. Just the basics. Then he tucked the equipment away. "I think you should let us take you to the hospital. Get your head checked out just to be sure it's not something to be concerned about."

"I promise I'll set up an appointment later if I start feeling any symptoms. But I didn't lose consciousness." For more than a few seconds. She hoped her smile would convince him.

She let her gaze roam the area around the burning house and then twisted around to look behind her.

Was the man responsible for the explosion watching them? The water hose spray drew her attention. Firefighters directed the hose at the burning house, but now and then a flame would crackle and shoot back up. The propane tank had blown too.

Again, the sensation that someone watched

her washed over her. Sadie hugged herself and rubbed her arms. Time to find Gage.

She left the ambulance to search for him. He wasn't going to be happy she'd followed him closer to the house and the action, and hadn't stayed behind for her own safety, as he would put it. But she felt safer with him.

She found him speaking with the sheriff and another deputy—the same guy who questioned her in the hospital. Deputy Crowley. He'd seemed nice enough at the hospital, but she wouldn't take the chance that he would send her away from the scene. Sadie hung back near one of their official vehicles, almost hidden, so she could catch some of their words, though with the fire hose and the residual ringing in her ears, she couldn't understand everything said.

"Miss Casings must have seen something or knew something and it cost her her life," the deputy said. "There was obviously something we missed in the house. At the time, her death appeared to be a drowning accident."

Gage had his hands on his hips and his back to Sadie. "I think we can all agree this must be big if someone went to these measures to destroy evidence."

The sheriff spoke up. "If that's true, and someone purposefully destroyed the house, it's likely connected with Miss Strand's search of the house and her subsequent abduction. With the house now destroyed, we can assume the evidence went with it. We should get a deputy over to the aunt's house to stand watch at all times. I'm concerned about Miss Strand's safety."

"You're not the only one. I agree that she needs protection." Gage suddenly twisted around and stared right at her, his gaze pinning her.

FIVE

When the sheriff's attention had flicked to something behind him, Gage had instinctively known Sadie had followed him.

Now he stared her down. Her crystal-blue, fear-filled eyes blinking up at him, he couldn't hold that stance for long. The crazy urge to hold her entered his head then slid down into his heart. He shook it off, but still softened his demeanor. Then he left Sheriff Garrison and Deputy Crowley standing there and went to Sadie, drawing from somewhere deep if he wanted to keep his tone firm. All he had to do was remind himself that if anything happened to her now, it was all on him.

"I thought I told you to go to the hospital in the ambulance. You know I would have come up there to get you." Though maybe he hadn't communicated that part. "You need to be thoroughly checked out. Besides, it's safer there."

Sadie backed away. "Special Agent Sessions,

you're not my boss. I didn't want to go. The EMT gave me the all clear."

"Right." He wasn't entirely sure he believed her about the EMT, but on her other comment, she was correct. He wasn't her boss. Still, she had no business here in the danger zone.

Deputy Crowley stepped closer. "Miss Strand, I'm afraid you can't be here. This is now officially a crime scene."

"I don't see any tape."

Okay, now. Those were the exact wrong words to say to Crowley. But Gage had brought her here. Since she knew Karon well, he'd wanted Sadie to point out anything that appeared out of the ordinary. Gage knew she'd wanted to show him the computer. But now it was obliterated—that is, if it even remained in the house. Maybe the perp had removed the evidence when he'd abducted Sadie.

Crowley, however, didn't like her response and his face inched closer to hers. "Once the fire is dead and the truck is out of there, we'll cordon it off with tape, but for now our presence is enough."

"Okay, okay." Gage pressed his hands on her shoulders. "I brought her with me to point out something she'd found in the house, and to look for discrepancies from her last visit. She stays."

"Oh, yeah? Care to share what that is?" Crowley's mood had seriously soured.

"Dial it down, Crowley," Sheriff Garrison said. "I'm sure Sessions has every intention of sharing everything he's learned so far now that we're investigating Miss Strand's abduction and reopening the investigation on Karon Casings's death. Likewise, we'll share anything we come across that falls into Coast Guard jurisdiction. I'll contact the state boys too."

Gage nodded his agreement and Crowley backed off.

Crowley seemed fine earlier but maybe now that he'd made a mistake on his initial look into Karon's death he decided to take his frustration out on everyone else. Gage could give Crowley a little grace. He'd been there himself.

"You know as much as I do. Oh, wait." Gage tugged the dolphin pendant out of his pocket and handed it over. "Sadie found this on the sinking boat. It was her friend Karon's, which puts her on that same boat. See if you can get this analyzed. It's just one more piece to connect Sadie and Karon to this investigation. With two unexplained deaths in two weeks and active drug runners along the coast in this area, we're working off the supposition that Karon's death is connected to the drug smuggling operation

I've been investigating, which means Sadie's attempted murder is also likely connected."

Crowley nodded and eyed Sadie. He likely would have said more but didn't want to speak freely in front of her. "So what happened to Agent Thompkins?"

"He's been assigned to Miller's investigation. We'll work the case from all angles to wrap it up quickly." He would have informed them sooner, but he'd only just found out himself. "And this time we hopefully won't miss anything."

Crowley seemed about to challenge Gage's remark, but the sheriff warned him off with a look.

Grace aside, Gage bit back derogatory words regarding Crowley's shoddy preliminary investigation, which had included searching the vacation rental home to see if he could find evidence of foul play, as suspected by Karon's mother. Likely Thompkins had simply taken Crowley's word for it that Karon's death was an accident. Without evidence of jurisdiction—indications that Karon's death pertained to her duties or she was killed while on a Coast Guard station, or her death was related to crimes falling under Coast Guard jurisdiction such as maritime drug runner—there wasn't much more he could do.

Still, an accident? Yeah, he'd keep biting his words back.

"Maybe you should take her home now, Sessions." Crowley's tone had turned condescending.

Gage threw up his hands in surrender. He wouldn't take the bait and get into it with this man. He let Crowley's jabs roll off him. "Your boss is right. We need to work together. I'm taking Sadie home then I'll be back."

Sadie shook her head. "I don't want to leave, Gage. This was where Karon had been staying before her death. Maybe… Maybe there's something left that will give us a clue. Something that wasn't destroyed. Or maybe she brought a keepsake with her. I wouldn't want to leave it in the ashes."

It wasn't like they could find anything until the fire had died and the ashes cooled. Or until the sheriff released the crime scene, but Gage leaned in to whisper. "You found something already, remember?"

Her eyes brightened, if only a little. "The dolphin."

He nodded. "We'll get it back, don't worry." He held out his hand and she took it. Together they left the scene. He'd wanted her on that ambulance and well away from here, but fat chance. He'd had every intention of searching the area for the man who most likely remained to watch what became of the house. To make sure whatever it was he'd tried to destroy—an item, a letter, a secret—remained hidden. But Gage would have to trust the sheriff's deputies who'd been assigned to search the woods surrounding the house to either find the man in the red cap or evidence he'd been here. Something they could use to identify him.

He opened the SUV door for her and she climbed in, tossing him a tentative smile. "Thanks."

"You're welcome." Once she drew her arms and legs completely into the cab, he shut the door then hiked around to his side.

Maybe part of him wanted to actively search the perimeter, but the other part was glad she'd stayed behind so he could watch over her. And maybe another part just plain wanted to be with her. Unfortunately, Sadie Strand had always had that effect on him.

No. Not again, Sessions. Not again. You absolutely can't sink and drown over this woman again.

Gage climbed into the SUV, his presence taking the chill out of the cab. He had this strange effect on her. She felt protected and safe when she was with him. Sadie didn't think it had a thing to do with the fact he was CGIS. The sheriff and his deputy didn't make her feel protected. So it had to be something about Gage. For the life of her, she couldn't remember this about him from the time she'd spent with him before.

Had he changed?

Or had she?

Likely they had both changed to some degree. Add to that, the loss of her best friend and Sadie's near-death experience had left her vulnerable and oversensitive. Getting over her friend's death would take years, if she ever did. Grief would overwhelm her if she let it, and right now, she was on a mission to find Karon's killer. Unofficially, of course. Gage had slightly different goals as CGIS, but the end result should be the same: Karon's killer brought to justice.

She wouldn't stop until that happened, and she was glad that Gage was the investigator to go through this with her. His presence was the silver lining in all this. She trusted him to see it through, and protect her too. With all the world traveling she'd done, she'd never once worried about her safety. Never thought the terror of someone wanting her dead would keep her company.

Strange that this unfamiliar sense of terror had happened to her in Coldwater Bay, where she'd grown up, and not some continent in another hemisphere. Even stranger, Gage was in this with her.

What if she had to go through this alone?

Thank You, God, for bringing Gage.

"What do we do next?" she asked. "Do you think there's anything left on the hard drive of the computer after the explosion?"

"You never know with something like that. If this guy even left the computer behind when he abducted you, I hope the sheriff will find it at least somewhat intact. I'll check into that. But you have to understand there's no 'we' in this investigation. I'm the investigator. You're the victim of a crime."

"I thought you were going to protect me? How can you protect me if I don't come with you?"

He ran a hand around his neck. "It's not usually done. But you have a point. What I'd like to do next is visit Karon's work. Ask questions there. Because with you out of the country, you don't know much about her day-to-day life, do you?"

"Right. And I don't think her mother saw her much during the week either, but they were close. Still, talking to her coworkers is a good plan. I can help you there if you don't already know. She worked at Rollins Environmental in Olympia."

"She's a conservationist then like her marine

biologist friend Sadie Strand, I take it." He shot
her a grin. "What did Karon do there?"

"She focused on hydrological aspects of crit-
ical areas. You know—wetlands, shorelines.
Rivers and streams. She assessed them for res-
toration."

"Any thoughts on why someone would want
to kill her? Any ideas at all?"

"I wish I knew, Gage. I tried to find out and
we saw what happened."

"Exactly why you shouldn't be investigating
on your own."

"I knew you'd come to your senses."

"What…what did I say? Oh now, wait, you
took that wrong. That wasn't some kind of in-
vitation."

"Wasn't it?" she teased.

The way his jaw worked as he drove, she
knew he was figuring it out. Then he glanced
over quickly before his attention went back to
the road. "I want to keep you close, Sadie, to
protect you, but not if it puts you in more danger."

"Thank you, Gage. I'm safer with you." *So let
me help.* But she wouldn't push him.

Normally, Sadie would continue the banter
and argue with him about her role in their unof-
ficial partnership, whatever it was, but the day
was well and truly catching up with her. Her

head pounded and a wave of nausea hit her, reminding her she'd been drugged and put on that
boat, left to drown. The doctor never told her
what had been used to drug her. She'd have to
remember to find out.

Sadie leaned against the headrest and closed
her eyes. A light, misty rain started falling.

"Gotta love Washington weather." Gage
turned on the windshield wipers.

Sadie woke up with a start. Her neck ached
from sleeping at an odd angle. "Where am I?"
she asked, as it all came back to her.

"You're in my SUV." His voice wrapped
around her.

"Oh, okay. Now I remember." She stretched.

Gage shifted into Park. "And we just arrived
at your aunt Debby's house."

"I can't believe I dozed off like that." She
shook off the sleep and disorientation.

"You needed the rest. You've been through
too much in one day." Gage turned off the ignition.

"As far as I know," she said, "you went
through most of it with me." He'd been in the
water with her and knocked down in the explosion.

"But I wasn't drugged and left cold and soaking for hours." Had his hazel eyes always been

this bright? "Are you sure you're okay? Don't need a doctor to check you over just to be safe?"

"Please, no more doctors. No more hospital." She reached for the handle.

"Oh, nope. Wait for me." He got out of the SUV and ran around to the other side to open the door for her.

Who does that anymore?

But she was halfway out of the passenger seat and stretching her legs toward the asphalt when dizziness swept over her. He caught her by the waist and set her down.

"See, I told you to wait." Gage's face twisted into a half frown.

Maybe his opening the door for her hadn't been about being a gentleman, but more about assisting her when he could see she wasn't feeling well. He didn't believe that she was okay.

"Even though it's summer, I'm chilled to the bone. All I want is to get warm in front of the fire." The home where she'd lived for years drew her attention. Her heart warmed with the familiar sight but unfortunately the warmth did nothing for the chill that had taken hold.

Aunt Debby stood on the porch of the simple home with tan vinyl siding and called to them. Sadie eyed Gage. "You know you have to come in."

"I really can't. I have to get back to the crime scene at the house."

"What happened to keeping me with you to protect me?"

"I will as much as I can, but you should be safe with your aunt for now. Just don't go anywhere alone. Keep the doors locked. You need to rest and I have a job to do. You want me to solve this, don't you?"

"Of course, but you can't hurt Aunt Debby's feelings. Just come in and say hi and then explain you need to get back to work. She always liked you, you know." Gage had lived in Jackson and she'd gone to school with him. She'd practically grown up with him, but they hadn't been close, hadn't been friends until college. Hard to believe she'd known him that long.

Gage chuckled. "Well, I always liked her too."

"So you coming in or what?"

"For five minutes."

Gage followed Sadie up the sidewalk and onto the porch. Aunt Debby hugged her. "It's such a chilly afternoon. Gage, you come in and have a cup of coffee."

"Don't mind if I do."

Aunt Debby headed for the kitchen as she gave them weather updates. Sadie showed Gage to an old sofa that had been there back when she'd hung out with him. He took a seat. "Four minutes and counting," he whispered.

Where should she sit? Next to Gage, or in the chair across the way, which seemed too far? But next to him seemed too close. Maybe she should help her aunt, but the woman had already returned with two cups of coffee. Sadie took one and wrapped her hands around the hot ceramic mug, and Aunt Debby handed the other to Gage.

"I wish you had gotten back about a half hour ago," Aunt Debby said. "You had an old friend stop by."

"What?" Sadie asked. "Who was it?"

"Oh, now let me see. He introduced himself but now I can't remember the name. I will, don't worry. He asked questions about you and said he wanted to catch up. Hadn't seen you since college. I thought he might have been a professor or something because he's older than you."

A chill crawled up Sadie's spine. She eased onto the sofa next to Gage. "What did he look like?"

"Tall like Gage. Slender. Pockmarked face. Listen to me. I remember that but not his name." Aunt Debby pressed her palm against her cheek as she tried to remember.

Tension corded Sadie's neck. "You need to be careful and not open the door to strangers. He could have pretended to know me. Remember, someone tried to kill me."

"Oh, my. I didn't even consider that."

"And there's something else. Gage and I went to Karon's vacation house. As we were approaching the house, someone wearing a red cap came out and ran away. And then the house exploded."

Aunt Debby gasped. "What? The house blew up? Oh, Sadie…" Tears choked back any more words.

Then the mug slipped from Aunt Debby's fingers and shattered on the floor. Her gaze lifted to meet Sadie's. "The man who stopped by. He wore a red cap too."

SIX

Debby appeared shaken to the core. Completely understandable. Gage knew how she felt.

"Maybe you should sit down." Gage moved to her side and assisted her into the chair.

"Tell me what happened," she said. "What's really going on here?"

He filled Debby in on what they knew so far, without all the gory details. "We can't know for sure that he rigged the explosion, but we need to question him if we can find him." Both to learn if he had anything to do with Karon's murder and Sadie's abduction, and if Gage could tie what happened to Karon to the drug smugglers for his investigation. More than that, Gage wanted to clamp down on all threats to Sadie.

"I'm scared, Gage. This man came to my home, looking for my niece so he could harm her? The audacity! The gall!" The lines in her fiftysomething face turned hard. "That infuriates me. Who does he think he is? This…this…

monster. I hope he comes back. I'd like to get my hands on him and show him what I think of him."

Uh-oh. Gage had better get control of the situation. He didn't need Debby thinking she was going to take justice into her own hands. That could put her in danger. "Please, just calm down. We don't want him coming back here, Debby. You are not to put yourself in harm's way under any circumstances." But he understood her fierce need to protect Sadie.

Her frown softened a bit, and concern flooded her gaze. Debby stood and paced then approached Sadie. "You can't stay here. He knows where to find you. You have to find someplace else to stay until the police catch this guy and stop him."

Now she was being reasonable.

"I agree with your aunt," Gage said. "And Debby, you should stay somewhere for a while too. You'll need to give a description of the man. I'll see if we can line up a forensic artist. But for now, let's get you somewhere safe."

He adjusted the miniblinds to better see outside. A deputy made his way up the sidewalk. Gage opened the door before he could knock and introduced himself.

"I'm here to watch the house and wanted to let the ladies know."

Debby inserted herself into the small space at the door. "Well, you're a day late and a dollar short. I've already had a dangerous man stop here and ask me questions. I probably told him more than I should."

The deputy appeared green to Gage. "Debby, let me handle this."

He went outside with the deputy and filled him in as they walked back to his department vehicle. "I'd like you to stay here and watch the house so our perpetrator will believe the ladies are still living here. That should buy us some time."

The deputy exaggerated a slow shake of his head. "I don't know if the sheriff is going to buy into that. I'm here to watch over people. Not an empty house."

"I'm sure he'll approve of it. Desperate times call for desperate measures. In fact, we can call him now, if you like. I'll talk to him myself."

The deputy handed Gage his cell after making the call.

Gage was surprised the deputy actually wanted him to do the talking. He shouldn't be. Like he thought, the guy was green. Surely the man could see the plan made sense.

Gage spoke to the sheriff and squared everything with him, then handed the cell off to the deputy.

He didn't have time for this. Back at the house, he found Sadie and Debby packing bags. He'd wanted to be on the road and back to the burning house to look for clues and search the woods where he'd seen the man flee. But with Debby's encounter with the man, everyone's plans had changed. Maybe he should let the deputy outside be both babysitter and watchdog, but this was Sadie and her aunt. Gage didn't trust them to anyone else. He'd see them somewhere safe. Once he dropped the women off, he could focus back on his investigation.

Debby lugged a big case over to the door.

"Looks like you're planning to stay for a while." He almost chuckled, but the situation was far too serious.

"I don't know how long this is going to take. And besides, what if he blows up my house too? I need a few things."

Images of the vacation house exploding, the concussive force slamming him and Sadie into the ground, ran through his mind. He didn't trust this guy not to do the same to Debby's home, except for one thing—Debby's home probably contained no evidence connecting ball cap guy to his crimes.

"Have you decided where you're going?" he asked.

Sadie entered, holding a small duffel bag.

"Since we're heading to Olympia to talk to people who worked with Karon, I think we should drop Aunt Debby at her brother Joe's house in Travis. It's on the way. Debby called Uncle Joe and he and his wife are expecting her."

"I know where it is." Gage gripped Debby's luggage and lifted it slightly off the floor to feel its weight. He sure hoped this didn't take as long as the woman was planning for. "And what about you, Sadie?" Gage knew the answer, but he had to ask anyway. "You could stay with them too."

Debby finished loading the dishwasher and turned it on. "I tried to talk her into it."

"I'll figure something out," Sadie said.

Right. She planned to stick close to his investigation.

And for Gage's part, how did he protect her and investigate at the same time? Maybe he was making a big mistake by keeping her close. Still, protective services wasn't completely out of the realm of CGIS responsibility. But that wasn't his official assignment here. His SAC would want Gage to do his part to protect her, of course. And he had a feeling she had memories locked away in that brilliant head of hers that would answer questions they didn't even know to ask.

If only that was the reason he wanted her

close. *Why, God? Why did you have to bring this woman back into my life?*

Half an hour later they dropped Debby off at her brother's home in Travis situated just outside of Olympic National Forest—one of his favorite places in the world. Another time and under much different circumstances, he might like to go hiking with Sadie for the sheer pleasure of seeing the sights—Sadie included. Why did his thoughts continually take him in the wrong direction? He once again shoved his unbidden romantic thoughts of Sadie away.

She hugged her family, who tried to talk her into staying. But she insisted she wouldn't rest until Karon's killer was caught as though she were officially investigating.

He kept any disparaging remarks he might have said to himself. Arguing with her wasn't a good use of his time.

Back in the SUV, Gage entered the information into the GPS for Karon's workplace—Rollins Environmental, Inc. "I think you might have missed your calling."

"How's that?"

"You should have joined the FBI or some other law enforcement entity so you could solve mysteries and bring justice to the world."

"I bring my own brand of justice. You can't believe the places I've been as I researched the aquarium fish trade. After that animated movie came out with a fish as the main character, suddenly every little kid wanted one. There's a long chain of suppliers between the source of those fish and the pet stores." Sadie went on to explain the decimated populations of the fish and the dangers posed to those harvesting them.

"Wow. I'm impressed. I remember you were always about conservation and protecting marine life. Justice for those who can't protect themselves. In fact, you did some real damage to that one company based on your discovery of pollutants that year."

"Yeah. I was interning at an environmental company. A different one from where Karon works. But just doing my job." She sighed as if pleased with the memory. "It was all in a day's work."

She'd always been driven. Even if they hadn't discussed it, he knew that she would investigate on her own if he didn't keep her at his side. Just one more reason to keep her close.

He liked that the conversation had given them a chance to reflect on the past and the good times. "Tell me, how does all that research bring justice? What can you do with it?"

"I have to educate people like I'm doing now." She turned her smile on him. "Will you buy fish for a tank in the near future?"

"I'd have to think twice about it, I admit." And he had considered having an aquarium to come home to since he couldn't keep a regular pet with his travel schedule. Still, maybe it wasn't all that bad, but he wouldn't argue the point with a conservationist.

"So see, I'm not new to complex investigations." Her voice suddenly cracked. "But I wasn't expecting something that would hit so close to home. I never dreamed I'd be searching for my best friend's killer."

Boy did he understand that. He could hardly believe he was here in the middle of it either.

She cleared her throat. "So how did you get where you are today, Gage?"

"Now there's a long and complicated story. I'm not sure I even remember." Nor did he want to. "Like you, I work to bring about justice, so I guess we have something in common."

"If you don't count our past. We have a past in common."

"Right, if you don't count that. I ended up in law enforcement and worked to build my resume. I worked on everything I could, getting as much experience as I could, working on violent crimes, terrorism cases. Even in foreign countries. In that time, I've seen entirely too much of the evil this world has to offer. Somehow—" he risked a glance at her "—and don't ask me how, I ended up back in Washington working for Coast Guard Investigative Services."

He was even up for promotion to the CGIS SAC when Jim left. "My parents were glad to have me back in Washington and close to home. I wanted to make them proud. But they died in an accident." The words brought back the morbid images.

"Oh, Gage… I didn't know. I'm so sorry." Sadie touched his arm.

An electric current charged with emotion surged all the way up his arm, across his chest and deep into his heart. His pulse increased, and he could have savored what her touch did to him. But instead he wished she would drop her hand. Finally, she did and he could breathe now.

He forced himself to bury the emotions she stirred in him and allowed the pain of the past— losing those he loved—to remind him to guard his heart from Sadie. Loving anyone too deeply could only bring heartache in the end.

"What happened?" she asked.

Could he even talk about it? "It's been two years, so not that long. It happened almost the same way it happened when the *Kraken* came across your sinking boat this morning." Had that only been this morning? "Only they were lost, and we couldn't save them."

"So... Is that why you jumped in for me against protocol?"

He couldn't answer so nodded, then finally said, "I can't get over the irony. I'm working for the Coast Guard and my parents drowned. They were right there. It could have ended differently." He struggled with his faith too. Where was God in all of this? Why did these things happen? Why, when he prayed every day of his life, did his parents die like that?

Another charge of electricity swept through him as Sadie pressed her hand against his arm to comfort him. She was a touchy-feely person, no doubt there. But could he survive his time with her? At least her comfort pushed away the morbid images for now.

"I'm sorry for your loss, Gage. Not that it will make you feel any better, but it's another thing we have in common now. I lost my parents in an accident too."

Why was she making a list? Between his crushes on Sadie in the past, he'd actually had a chance to fall in love with someone else. But that love had died a miserable death. Colleen had broken his heart.

And as far as Sadie was concerned, he'd failed at love twice with her already—though it hadn't been an actual reciprocating romantic relationship. He was so pathetic.

He wasn't about to buy all the bunk about a third time around, especially with Sadie Strand. Years ago the woman had never looked at him twice, always seeming to be attracted to Coasties—men serving in the Coast Guard. He couldn't help the half smile that slid into his lips. He realized to his chagrin that she might consider him a Coastie now—and perhaps that explained the change in the way she looked at him—but he would make sure to clarify that for her.

"Just to remind you, I'm a civilian agent. I'm not officially in the Coast Guard."

"You've accomplished so much, and you're a special agent, for crying out loud. You should be proud of everything you've done."

He hadn't meant it that way—as though he wasn't pleased with his accomplishments—but explaining to her why he'd brought it up wasn't an option.

Oh, now. What was she doing? As far as Sadie was concerned, the handsome CGIS special agent next to her might as well be a Coastie, and she'd sworn off men in the Coast Guard. They traveled too much, and her heart had been broken once too often. Nope. Not for her. Except, well, now that she thought about it—Sadie traveled a lot too in her research. In that case, she shouldn't let herself fall for anyone. After her experiences with men, she had too many trust issues. It was just too complicated.

Gage steered into the Rollins Environmental parking lot and found a spot between two vehicles. Sadie's palms grew moist. "Do you know what questions you're going to ask and who you're going to talk to?"

He reached over and patted her leg. "If you can't be good you'll have to stay in the car." Then he shifted back in his seat. "This is my investigation. You can come in with me but let me do the talking. Agreed?"

"Agreed."

"You can pretend you're on a research trip and simply observing. I'm sure you know how to do that."

"I do, so stop worrying."

Inside the compound, Gage introduced himself, revealing his official CGIS badge. The security guard at the marbled counter arched a brow.

"I need to speak with employees who worked with Karon Casings."

The man scrunched his face. "Is everything all right?"

"No, everything isn't all right. She was murdered," Sadie said.

Gage's eye flicked to her in warning.

The guard stood. "I knew she'd been on vacation and heard the news that she'd drowned. But murder?"

"We're investigating. If you wouldn't mind keeping that information to yourself for now. Did you know her well? Anything you can tell us?"

The guard shook his head. "I didn't know her personally. Just that she worked here. I'm sorry I can't help. But if I see anything…you know… suspicious, I can give you a call."

"Fair enough." Gage handed over his card. "Now if you'll please point us in the right direction."

The security guard's friendly demeanor had turned somber with the news. "Let me call personnel for you."

"I'd rather just talk to a few of her coworkers without making a stir. Can you arrange that?"

The guard set the phone back on the rest, his mouth in a resigned frown. "Sure. Take the elevators up to the third floor. Her office was the second one down to the right. Her stuff is still intact, I think. Nobody's had the heart to touch it. You can talk to her coworkers."

Gage nodded his thanks. Once in the elevators alone, Sadie spoke up. "Should her office be cordoned off as a crime scene?"

"Not unless there's evidence that points to her

being murdered there, then being moved to..." He let his words trail off. "But if given permission, then I have every intention of looking through her things in addition to questioning her coworkers. If Crowley hasn't already been here—and from the security guard's reaction, I don't think he has—then I'll share what I find, if anything."

The elevator door dinged open. Sadie went straight to Karon's office but the door was locked. Great. Gage moved down to the next office and softly knocked on a half-opened door.

A redheaded woman looked up from her computer. "Can I help you?"

Gage introduced himself again as well as Sadie. "I'm here to talk to you about your coworker Karon Casings."

She sucked in a breath.

"May we come in?"

"Certainly. Come in and sit down. My name is Shana Wilson." The woman came around her desk to close the door then sat back down. "Please tell me what's going on. We learned that she died in a drowning accident. Is that right?"

"We have reason to believe her death wasn't an accident."

"You mean—"

"She was murdered." Sadie cut Shana off. Oops. Gage wouldn't be happy at her intrusion, but he didn't give her a warning look. Still, if she expected him to let her tag along, she'd better not say another word.

"Murdered? But why? And by whom?" Unshed tears pooled in her eyes. "That's silly of me. Of course that's why you're here. You're trying to find out. How can I help?"

"We're hoping to find someone who knew her beyond just the office and maybe answer a few questions."

"That would be me. She had other friends here as well, but we were relatively close. She'd wanted me to go on her vacation with her, but I couldn't get the time off. Still, she had…secrets."

"Go on," Gage said.

Shana rose from her desk and went to the closed door. She peeked out into the hallway, then shut the door behind her again. "I wish we could have this conversation somewhere else, but that might raise suspicions."

Sadie wanted to speak up. Shana clearly knew something that could help them. Why hadn't she reported this to the police or the sheriff or someone?

She remained at the door as though gauging if anyone stood there to listen. What had her spooked?

Shana lowered her voice to a whisper. "Karon

had taken the two-week vacation, yes, but she came in after hours during her vacation to test a water sample. I thought it was odd at first, but she acted like it wasn't a big deal. I assumed she wanted to test the water where she was staying for some reason. I only knew because I'd been working late and had to rush home, so I didn't get to ask her more. The next thing I knew, she was found dead."

"Did you tell police what you've told us?"

Realization seemed to grip Shana as a tear slid down her cheek. "I haven't talked to the police. No one came here to ask questions. Her mother called to talk to her boss and tell him she had drowned."

"Why didn't you mention this to the police on your own?"

"Because I didn't realize there was any suspicion about her death. It had been a week since she'd come in for that test. I honestly never thought about it again. Not until you walked in here and said the word *murder*."

Sadie shuddered. Rubbed her arms.

Shana focused on Sadie. "You were her friend, weren't you? Are you the one who was in Indonesia on a research trip?"

Smiling, Sadie nodded.

Shana returned the smile. "She told me all about you. I'm glad you're back and you're here now to help them find out who killed her. I still don't understand why."

"If you could find out about the test results on the water sample she brought in," Gage said, "maybe that will give us information we can use. There might be a connection."

Shana's eyes grew wide. "Oh, right. Maybe I can help you with that."

"While you're looking into it, mind if we take a look in Karon's office? It was locked."

Nodding quickly, Shana rose and moved to the door to peek out. "I only have a key because Shana and I were close and we looked out for each other. Okay, the coast is clear."

Why would the coast need to be clear? Sadie wanted to ask that, but she let Gage do the talking. They followed Shana to the next office. Shana's hands trembled as she jiggled the key into the lock and opened the door. "I'm going back to my office to look up some files. If I can't find the information you need there, I'll have to go down to the lab. So wait for me in my office, okay?"

"Mind if I talk to some other of her coworkers?" Gage asked.

Frowning, she hesitated before responding. "I wouldn't do that just yet. Wait until I get back."

"What's going on here?" A man stood in the doorway. "What are you doing in Miss Casings's office? No one should be in here."

SEVEN

At the panicked look on Shana's face, Gage quickly stepped up to diffuse the situation. He flashed his badge. "I'm CGIS Special Agent Sessions. We're here to ask questions about Karon Casings."

"Why wasn't I informed of this?" The thirtysomething man lifted his shoulders higher. Definitely cocky and arrogant.

"Who are you exactly?" Gage asked.

"I'm Denver Epson, Karon's boss. You should have gone through human resources."

Gage didn't want to argue with the man and probably should redirect him, but he couldn't help himself. "Why on earth for? Unless someone in human resources knows something pertaining to Karon's murder? I'm not applying for a job. I'm investigating Karon's death."

Epson visibly paled. "Murder?" He glanced at Shana then back to Gage. "But I... I thought..."

Gage waited for him to finish what he would say.

"We heard she drowned." He fell back against the wall. "Who would do something like that?"

"That's what we're here to find out. Will you excuse me for a second? I need to have a word with my colleague." He pulled Sadie out of the office and down the hall. "I'm going to talk to this guy and while he's distracted, would you get the water sample or the results from Shana?"

Sadie scrunched her face. "Why don't you just ask him?"

"Obviously Karon didn't want anyone to know about it. She came up here at night. And Shana acts wary. I want to see what it is before too many more people know about it. Otherwise the likelihood it could get destroyed or tampered with will increase."

"Good idea." Sadie nodded and approached Shana, drawing her away from her boss.

Epson's demeanor had changed and he became more than willing to help. But the interview with him didn't reveal anything suspicious or out of the ordinary. The guy saw Karon at work and that was it, according to him. He seemed truly distraught that she had died, and especially upset to hear about the cause of death. But maybe the guy was a good actor. Gage talked to a couple of more employees that Epson said knew Karon, and then he donned gloves and searched her office for anything that might connect her to the drug runners or to her murderer, but found nothing. Either Karon had been extremely careful and diligent to leave nothing evidential behind, or there was nothing here to find. Crowley had mentioned calling in the state boys on this, so he'd leave them to decide if cordoning off her office was warranted, and instructed Epson to leave everything as it was, for now. Interesting the company had left her office intact even after two weeks. Someone certainly could have removed evidence during that time.

Gage went in search of Sadie, hoping she'd gotten the results of the water test, and found her alone in Shana's office.

She sat in a chair reading a magazine and slapped it closed when she saw him. "Are you ready to go?"

He leaned close and lowered his voice. "Did you get the goods?"

Without a direct answer, Sadie stood and grabbed his arm. She led him down the hall until they were out of Shana's general work space. "I'll explain when we're out of here."

He slowed up until she couldn't make him budge. "I'm not going anywhere without it."

"Yes, you are," she whispered. "Do you trust me or not?"

Fists on his hips, he said, "I could just go back and ask for it."

Sadie looped her arm through his and tried to encourage him forward. "I think we both know it's not that simple."

Gage acquiesced and together they exited the building. Neither of them spoke again until they were at his SUV.

"This had better be good." He tugged the keys out and unlocked the doors.

Once inside, he started the vehicle and waited. Sadie buckled her seat belt. Buying herself time to come up with a good explanation?

Her chest rose with her deep breath then fell again before she looked at him with her crystal-blue eyes. They could do him in if he let them. But he had to keep eye contact. "Well?"

"Shana was afraid to look for it. Or even go down to the lab. She didn't want her boss to see. So she'll give it to us later."

Gage reached for the door. Sadie gripped his bicep. He really wished she wouldn't do that. He turned to face her as she leaned on the console, putting her face much closer to his. Her pretty lips formed a soft smile. "Gage, listen. If she meets us later, she is more likely to give us additional information, don't you think?"

The woman made a good point. "But she could also destroy the test results. Maybe she doesn't want us to see those. And you just risked our chance to get them."

"Oh, come on, she wouldn't have brought that up if she didn't want us to know." Sadie edged away from the console, putting distance between them, and leaned against the seat.

That was better. She wasn't so close, but Gage found himself wishing for her nearness again. He focused back on task. "True. There must be something more to tell because she was definitely nervous about being seen talking to us. Did she say when and where she would meet us?"

"Tomorrow morning in Vickson. There's a little mom-and-pop restaurant. Can't remember the name."

"Why there?"

"Because I didn't think you'd want to drive all the way back here to Rollins in Olympia tomorrow. Vickson is halfway between Coldwater Bay and Olympia. I forgot that I'm not staying with Aunt Debby so that I could stay anywhere. We could have stayed in Olympia, even. I didn't think about it at the time."

"That's fine." Gage nodded and steered from the Rollins Environmental parking lot. He needed to speak with Deputy Crowley. Gage hadn't learned much of anything yet. Until they saw the results of the water sample to dis-

cover what Karon was looking into, they had
no idea if it was connected to her murder or to
Gage's drug runners. If it was connected, there
could be a motive buried in there somewhere.
Gage couldn't help but wonder what investigative angle Deputy Crowley was taking, since
he hadn't visited Karon's employer. Still, Gage
would call him after they met with Shana in
the morning.

"We'll head that way then and find someplace to get a couple of rooms, unless you want
to go back to Coldwater Bay. It's not that far.
You never told me where you were planning to
stay to be safe. I still vote for your uncle Joe's
with your aunt."

"Maybe I will end up there. But I'm kind
of hoping we can find the guy who did this to
Karon before I have to move in with Uncle Joe
and Aunt Neta along with Aunt Debby."

He kept his attention focused on the two-lane
road that snaked around the mountains, hedg-
ing a deep gorge on one side. His shoulder and
neck muscles grew tense. He didn't feel as if
he'd gained any ground at all. How was it all
connected? Karon, Sean, Sadie and the maritime drug runners? Who was the man who'd
questioned Debby? There was much more going
on here, and he needed to catch a break while
keeping Sadie safe.

"Don't forget it's not only about finding Karon's killer—but someone tried to kill you. You have to stay alert."

"Don't worry. I'll never forget."

Without thinking about it, Gage reached over and put his hand over Sadie's on the console between them. She didn't pull away. *What are you doing, man?* He'd never done this when they had hung out in college. Never put his hand over hers in a tender way. Comforted her when she'd gotten her broken heart, sure, but this was purely impulsive on his part.

"I hope this will end soon and then one day you can truly put this behind you," he said.

"Me too, Gage, me too. But there's one part of this I don't want to put behind me."

"Oh, what's that?" His heart skipped a little at her tone.

"I'm glad we reconnected. I'm glad you're in this with me. I wouldn't want anyone else. I'm not sure I could even trust anyone else with my safety as much as I do you."

The weight of that responsibility pressed on him already, and her words heaped more pressure on him. Gage wasn't sure how to react or what to say. He'd warned himself away from this woman. She'd never once looked at him in "that way," but now her tone, her words, had his heart tumbling all over.

Lights from the vehicle behind them flashed in his rearview mirror, approaching them much too fast. "Hold on!"

Gage tried to accelerate, but it was too late. The vehicle rammed into the back of his SUV.

The force threw her forward, the seat belt holding her body in place, but her screams escaped.

The SUV fishtailed. Gage corrected and accelerated. She risked a glance his way. Caught the deep furrows of his face and his tight jaw. His iron grip on the wheel and tensed body.

His demeanor added to her terror. Her heart would crash through her rib cage.

"What's going on?" Stupid question.

"You know as much as I do." His brows dove even lower.

She hoped for some reassurance, but that had been a long shot. As Gage accelerated, driving much too fast for comfort on a curvy mountain road, she gulped for breath and sent up continuous silent prayers for help and protection.

She thought she might hyperventilate. *Someone wants me dead. Someone doesn't want me to find the truth out about why Karon was murdered.*

But they weren't going to scare her away. She wouldn't give up. She would never give up until justice was served. She just hoped Gage wasn't in more danger because of her.

Tires squealed as he whipped the SUV around a corner, the vehicle leaning precariously to the side. Sadie held on to the handgrip with all her strength. Tried to steady her breathing. On the right side, beyond the guardrail, the road dropped down a hundred feet or more into a ravine, crystal clear water flowing out of Olympia National Forest. She couldn't see that now since dusk had fallen, but knew it was there.

"I need you to call 9-1-1 for me. I can't take my hands off the wheel."

"My cell is in my bag and that's down on the floorboard. I can't reach it without unbuckling."

"Don't do that. Just use mine."

She snatched his cell and hoped for some bars. Got one, but that would have to do. Sadie entered the numbers...

The vehicle slammed them from behind.

And the cell flew from her hands onto the floorboard. "Oh, no, Gage. I dropped the phone." She reached for her seat belt.

"Do. Not. Under any circumstances, release your restraint. That could get you killed."

"I'm such an idiot!"

"You're not. It's not your fault. Just pray. Trust God, and trust that He'll give me the means to get us out of this."

Sadie nodded and sent up a prayer. She still felt like an idiot.

The other vehicle pulled up next to them on the two-lane mountain road. She glanced over her shoulder and could barely make out another SUV— full-size. Maybe a Suburban. No wonder the driver was so bold and aggressive. He had the bigger vehicle.

Gage accelerated again to try to pull ahead but the other vehicle kept pace with them.

"Gaaaagge…" Her pitch rose as she said his name. She grasped her armrest on the left, and the grip at the top of the door to her right as though her efforts would save her life if they crashed.

The pursuing vehicle on the left swerved toward them and bumped them over the gravel shoulder. Gage tried to steer back onto the road.

"Why aren't your airbags working?"

"They're designed to go off in a frontal crash. The vehicle behind us might have disengaged theirs, considering they just rammed us."

"They're trying to run us off the road." Sadie could hardly think of anything more terrifying—except waking up on a sinking boat. "You know what that means, right? There's nowhere for us to go except into the ravine. You can't let them do that."

Gage said nothing at all, which was fine with

her. Maybe he was so focused he hadn't even heard her. She'd let him concentrate on getting them out of this. He overcorrected intentionally and slammed into the bigger SUV then suddenly slowed. Their pursuer pulled ahead. Gage sped up until the front wheels of his SUV aligned with the back wheels of the bigger vehicle, then he steered toward the back side and gently bumped it. The other vehicle started skidding and whipped around and off the road to the left.

"That was a messed-up version of the PIT maneuver. You've heard of that—the police often use it to force a fleeing car to stop." Gage increased speed, leaving their pursuer behind.

"Aren't you going to stop and get out? Use your weapon and apprehend the guy?"

"Not with you in the car. I don't know how many are in the vehicle or what kind of ammunition they brought. He or she or they could be loaded for bear. If you weren't with me, sure, I'd risk it. But keeping you safe is more important."

"So you're going to let them get away just to protect me?"

"Protecting life is always my priority. Especially when it's yours."

What did he mean by that? Any other time and Sadie might have let herself ponder his words. But headlights from two vehicles half a mile up headed their way. More trouble? Or passersby that could be put in harm's way? "I hope this doesn't cause those drivers any trouble."

Oh, Lord, this is so awful. Please help us!

Gage stared into the rearview mirror. "Our pursuer is coming for us again." Gage accelerated and whipped the vehicle around a curve in the mountain road.

Sadie once again held on tight. "Gage, slow down! It's dark out. You can't see where you're going!"

"Then neither can he." Keeping his focus on the road, he ground out the words.

"You can't race him, you can't outrun him. You're going to get us killed."

"I'm going to save our lives. Save *your* life." He slowed the vehicle.

"What…what are you doing?"

"We lost him for now. We have about five seconds before he makes that curve." The tires screeched on a hard stop. "Now get out."

"What?"

"Just do it! Get over by that rock and hide. Do not move from that spot."

She hesitated as she tried to wrap her mind around his plan.

"Two seconds left. Hurry."

She jumped out and scrambled in the dark

over to the boulder edging the shoulder. "I hope you meant this one," she mumbled.

Then he took off again. "Gage!" Wait. Where was he going?"

Oh, Lord, please protect him. She had thought he would get out with her and they were leaving the vehicle to roll on its own or parked at the side of the road so their pursuer would crash into it. But that hadn't been Gage's plan at all.

The pursuing vehicle sped around the curve, giving chase. Oh, no. She couldn't stand by and watch this. Why had she gotten out of the vehicle in the first place? She would rather be with Gage right now—then he might be more protective of himself in order to keep her safe.

But he'd given her precious few seconds to get out or even question him on his plan. Sadie paced near the boulder next to the road, watching the scene unfold before her. She could only see the rear lights of both vehicles, hear tires squealing and engines roaring.

I can't stand this!

If only she'd brought her cell with her, she could call 9-1-1. But she hadn't had a chance to think.

Pulse pounding in her ears, Sadie pressed her back against the cold boulder. Gage had put her safely out of the way to risk his life and stop whoever had tried to run them off the road.

God, please help him. Please save him. She squeezed her eyes shut and prayed hard. The sound of cars slowly driving by in the opposite lane drew her attention and she opened her eyes. A car slowed, probably either calling the police about the two crazies on the road or watching what would happen.

In horror, Sadie watched the bright red rear lights of the two vehicles in combat down farther.

Gage against the giant. Tires screeched. Metal crunched. One of the vehicles rolled over and over...

And over.

"No! Gage!" Her cry echoed through the night.

EIGHT

Gage shook off the daze. Dragged in a ragged breath. *I'm alive.*

He let that fact sink in as he stared through his cracked windshield at the dark forest, partially illuminated by the headlights. They had surprisingly remained on despite the crash. Stiff, he released the seat belt and pain stabbed across his chest. The seat belt restraining him had both bruised him and saved his life.

The airbags had deployed this time due to the frontal impact when he'd collided with the other driver. But he'd gone through a second collision. A huge tree branch pierced the passenger-side door.

Oh, God...

If Sadie had been there...

He couldn't even think about it. The rest of the vehicle's damage he couldn't see in the dark. He twisted slightly and from where he sat, it looked like the vehicle's back end had struck a tree.

That could have been a deadly impact. But Gage had survived. He doubted his SUV had fared as well as Gage, though he'd feel it tomorrow.

He hung his head, taking it all in. *Thank You for protecting me, God.*

The other vehicle had flipped a few times. Had its occupants survived? Gage tried to open his door but it wouldn't budge. The frame had buckled. He climbed over into the back, squeezing through the crushed metal and kicked *that* door opened. The hinges squeaked and it fell off and tumbled to the ground.

Gage carefully stepped from his SUV, noting it was precariously twisted against the tree. His gut tensed and his knees shook. But he didn't have time to comprehend the wreck—to some degree, he'd asked for it when he'd battled the pursuer, but he'd had no choice but to battle or surrender to certain death.

Now…he had to finish this once and for all. He moved around to the passenger side, fighting the devastating image that came to mind had Sadie remained with him, and dug around the floorboard for his phone. His fingers touched something—his cell!—and he urged it closer and snatched it up.

Pulling his firearm out from his shoulder holster, he held it at temple index ready—muzzle up at the side of his head. With his free hand, he used his cell to call for backup and emergency services as he approached the other vehicle, which had rolled several times and now rested upside down. Fortunately, the headlights continued to shine, as well, and would warn approaching vehicles there'd been a wreck. Good thing this wasn't a frequently traveled road, but on the other hand, a busier road could have prevented their pursuer's bold attack in the first place.

He might take time to place additional warning markers, but he needed to check on the driver of the other vehicle, which had stopped rolling smack in the middle of the highway.

It could have gone right off the edge.

God, please let them still be alive. Apprehending whoever had attacked them tonight could end this or at least give them answers that would lead them to Karon's murderer and Sadie's abductor. Funny how his main mission and purpose for this investigation was to find out what the two incidents had to do with his maritime drug runners investigation but all he could think about was protecting Sadie.

Headlights from other vehicles on the road appeared a couple of miles out. They'd be here in under a minute. He didn't want to get into a gun battle on the road. Someone else could get hurt. He hoped Sadie had remained at the boulder like he'd instructed her so she would be safe—he'd go back to get her when this was over, but he didn't want her anywhere near this scene and so close to whoever wanted her dead.

Lowering his firearm to low ready, he carefully crept toward the vehicle, uncertain what he would find. An assailant waiting to shoot him down in the street? An injured person or a body?

He hoped he'd find only one person and that person wouldn't be too injured for Gage to assist him out. He wanted information and he wanted it now. Who had abducted Sadie and was still trying to kill her—and now Gage too—and why? Who had killed Karon? He shoved down the fury and focused.

From this side, he couldn't see anyone in the vehicle. He continued around to the other side. Other cars approached and slowed. There was no way they could make their way around this mess until the authorities arrived to clear it. Bracing himself, he crouched low to peer inside, his heart pounding.

And found the driver's seat empty.

As well as the passenger's side. He crouched lower and looked in the back.

That meant their assailant had escaped. The airbags had deployed so maybe his or her injuries weren't severe.

Sadie...

Now his advice to her to remain hidden at the rock didn't seem like such a great idea. Gage wanted to kick himself.

God, please...please keep her hidden and safe!

He gauged the distance back to that rock. Was she still there and hiding? He needed to go find her. But he also needed to remain at the scene of the accident. There was no way her assailant knew he'd dropped her off back there.

No way.

Still.

Gage made his decision. Sadie was his priority. He hiked up the road, leaving behind the wreck and a line of cars.

Emergency sirens blared, growing louder. Good. They could take care of the mess, though they would wonder about the two empty vehicles. But his goal was to find Sadie to make sure she was safe.

I never should have left her!

He'd had no choice. He'd keep reminding himself. He had to leave her somewhere safe.

But in leaving her, he had also put her at risk. He jogged up the incline. Would she see him and head toward him? As he grew closer to the rock, a sense of dread engulfed him.

It was quiet. Too quiet. He would have expected to hear her say something by now. Admittedly, he loved the way she said his name. *Come on, Sadie, let me hear you say my name.* Or if he didn't hear her voice, he would expect to at least see her athletic form appear, her hair shining in the moonlight.

Gasping for breath after his rush up the hill, he reached the rock. Marched around it.

She wasn't there.

"Sadie! Where are you?"

Nor was she on the road heading toward the crash.

His heart dropped to his gut. Gage positioned his weapon, used a flashlight and searched for the sign of a struggle.

But saw none. Obviously something had happened, but what?

Jesus, please don't let her be in trouble. Please, help me to help her! "Sadie!"

A Washington State Trooper vehicle pulled up next to him, shining bright lights. The troopers jumped out and pointed their weapons at him. "Put your weapon down!"

Oh, no, no, no, this wasn't how this was supposed to go.

But Gage was no fool to argue with them. He

did exactly as he was told and set the gun on the ground. "I'm Special Agent Sessions with CGIS. I called for backup. Please allow me to show you my badge."

The officers approached, but kept their weapons at the ready. Gage handed over his credentials. "We don't have much time here. I'm looking for the woman who was with me and also our attacker. The SUV driver. He escaped. I need your help."

Gage hated taking the time to explain everything that had happened, but once he obtained the officers' full cooperation, that would mean more people searching. That was for the best. Wasn't it? He'd forget about the time lost. Now that a host of law enforcement and emergency workers had arrived, the light traffic on this lone highway had begun to move again.

"You don't think she ended up down there, do you?" The older trooper shined his flashlight over the edge.

Gage's gut tensed. "I hope not. I don't even want to think like that. Let's search the woods. If she'd felt threatened, she would have run to the woods to hide."

"Why not toward the accident and where she could find you?"

"Maybe she wanted to, but she couldn't."

The troopers agreed, and they all headed

toward the dark woods of Olympic National Forest—the beauty of moss and twisted vines would be lost on them in the dark. Through trees, flashlights beamed and voices called.

And the entire time he tried to hold onto hope that she was still alive, the truth burned a hole in his heart. He'd failed what had quickly become his primary mission—keeping Sadie safe.

Oh, God, I've lost her...

Branches whipped her face and she stumbled on gnarly roots and slipped on moss in the temperate rain forest. Olympic National Forest— she never dreamed she'd be running for her life through such a beautiful place. If she survived this, could she ever enjoy the forest again?

Gasping for breath, she refocused on one thing: getting away.

Have to keep going. Have to keep running.

Literally fleeing for her life, she relied solely on the moon, which barely filtered through the dense canopy, if at all, to guide her way. She headed west and tried to remain parallel to the highway until she could turn and run into the road where the accident had happened. All those emergency vehicles that were sure to have arrived along with the law enforcement could keep her safe.

Except she had the feeling that she'd gotten

lost, despite her efforts to remain oriented. She'd trekked north and should have intersected the road by now, but it wasn't there. She couldn't see the emergency lights through the thick woods. Couldn't hear the sirens or law enforcement voices. Had she gotten disoriented, after all?

A panicked whimper threatened to escape.

Gage, where are you?

When she'd heard the sound of metal crunching, the clash of two vehicles as the two SUVs collided and bounced off one another—one of them flipping and the other skidding into the woods, she'd feared the worst. What if Gage had been killed? People had died in less-dramatic accidents.

All she could think about was Gage. Getting to Gage. How could she wait for him when she had no idea if he would even come? He could be injured or dying without her help. She could search for the cell phone in the wreckage and finally make that call for help.

Without a second thought, she'd left the hiding place behind the rock to go check on the accident and see if he was injured.

Sadie had plodded along the shoulder, praying and trying to shove back the tears so she could be strong and do what needed to be done. That's when she'd heard the grunts of a man half limping and half jogging up the road.

At first she'd thought it was Gage coming for her, but right before she called out and exposed herself, the moonlight had revealed that it wasn't him at all. It was someone else.

Was it just a random stranger—a vagrant hiking the road?

She doubted it. Realization had taken much too long to dawn when it finally hit her this could be the man after her—he'd crawled out of his wrecked vehicle and was now trying to escape Gage...or did he actually know where she'd hidden? No. That couldn't have been it.

But if she didn't find a place to hide, he would walk right into her because he headed straight for her. Had he seen her yet? But if she moved, he was sure to see her then before his path intersected where she stood.

She'd had two choices. The woods across the road, the Olympic National Forest, or the rocky cliff just beyond the boulder where she'd hidden.

Right. There had been only one choice. She'd taken off into the woods. She'd planned to make her way around back to the wreck so she could check on Gage and also call for help.

But the man had seen her.

He'd followed her into the woods! That had left no doubt who he was. What an idiot she'd been. Still, life hadn't given her any good choices.

As she continued running and dragging in enough breath to keep up with her frantic heart, the man had been closing in on her. She could not believe how fast a limping man could move, but he'd kept up with her and even gained ground, and now sheer terror kept her running without a clue which direction she went.

She should have found the road by now. Should see something or somebody who could help. Now what was she going to do?

Pausing next to a tree, she leaned over and sucked in a breath. Sweat coated her back and ran down her face, even in the cool night. She peered behind her. The sound of branches snapping and bushes being trampled met her ears. A large animal would have made less noise.

What do I do? I don't know what else to do. I can't keep running...

If Gage had survived that wreck, then he would find her. She had to believe he'd survived.

Just get away. Get as far away as you can.

She stumbled forward and hit the ground hard. Pain shot up her knees. Her breaths came hard and fast. She'd made too much noise. She scooted over to a large gnarly tree to hide. Waited and listened.

Crunch...crunch, crunch...crunch, crunch.

The limping man.

"I know you're there." The man's breathing rasped.

Sadie kept silent. He wanted to taunt her so she'd give herself away. She wouldn't take the bait. But her breathing was far too loud. She held her breath, but her lungs burned, screaming for more oxygen.

The crunching, limping footfalls drew nearer to the gnarly tree.

Her heart pounded. She couldn't control her panic. Palms sweating, she felt around for something with which to defend herself. But…nothing. There was nothing. Squeezing her eyes shut, she pressed her head against the tree back and willed herself to be invisible.

He was close, so close. She could hear him. Feel him. The hackles on her neck raised.

God, please let me be invisible. Please don't let him find me in here.

Her heart pounded so hard, so loud in her ears, she was sure the man could hear it in the quiet forest.

Then, she heard his breathing. Had she imagined his hot breath against her cheek, causing her hair to tickle her face? If she waited one more second, he would grab her, he was that close.

Sadie had to make a run for it. Again, life gave her no choices.

Shoving from the tree, she pushed off to make a mad dash, but pain rippled over her head when he caught her by the hair and jerked her back against him. He wrapped his arms around her and pinned hers against her, so she couldn't fight or hit him. But she could kick and scream—and she gave it all she had.

Screamed as loud as she could.

"Who are you? What do you want from me?"

He whispered into her ear, "Everything."

Shouts came from somewhere in the woods—which direction, she wasn't even sure anymore. Didn't care.

"Over here!" she screamed.

He shoved her onto the ground, smashing her face into the forest floor of ferns and moss. "I will kill you here and now if you do that again."

He could have killed her then had her head hit that rock.

Hope surged.

A rock!

She reached for it. Wrapped her fingers around it, hoping it wasn't half buried in the dirt. The man hefted her up to carry her off. Sadie twisted around and slammed the rock into his temple. He dropped her. Stumbled forward. She didn't wait around for him to recover and ran toward the voices. "Help! I'm over here!"

More voices resounded. Flashlights beamed.

Sadie ran toward them. Relief fueled her every step. All she had to do was find them before he grabbed her again. This time he likely would kill her.

"Hey!" Someone shouted from much too close. Strong arms pulled her around and against a hard chest.

Oh, no! He caught her again! "Help!"

She fought to get free, but he grabbed her wrists and held them tight. "Sadie, it's me. It's me!"

It finally registered that the familiar, handsome face, and the comforting voice, belonged to Gage. Only his face appeared haggard, and his voice had sounded distraught.

She released a long sigh and practically collapsed against him.

"Gage. Oh, Gage…"

He hugged her to him. Wrapped his arms around her. "I thought I'd lost you—" his voice cracked "—I thought I'd lost you," he said, softer then. "I'm so sorry."

"And I thought you'd been hurt in the wreck, or even killed. I couldn't know." A sob broke free. "I had to go check on you and then he came after me. He's back there. The man… someone should go after him."

Releasing her, Gage held her at arm's length. "What happened?"

"He tried to take me. I hit him in the head. You'd better hurry if you're going to get him. He has a limp—maybe he was injured in the wreck—but it doesn't slow him down that much."

The search party approached. Gage explained their attacker was in the woods and had a limp. Deputies and a few troopers took off into the woods. They'd likely call in park rangers on the manhunt, as well.

"Let's get you home." Gage moved to carry her in his arms. "Though I'm not entirely sure where that is."

"No, it's okay. I can walk." But Sadie wished she hadn't said the words. What would it feel like for Gage Sessions to carry her in his strong arms? Against his broad chest? She'd be so close to his face and would rest her head against his shoulder, safe and secure. It would feel entirely too good. And that's why she absolutely had to extricate herself from his proximity.

But later. Much later. She could at least walk as close to him as possible. After the close call on both their lives, she would soak up the comfort he offered. They were friends, after all, and could handle this. Still, something in her heart had shifted toward him about the time he pulled her from the ocean. The guy was her hero. In fact, considering he'd saved her life, she might even consider him on par with superheroes. But she couldn't let herself fall into the hero-worship trap—fall in love—like Gwen Stacy with Spiderman.

That didn't end well.

NINE

He tugged her close and guided her through the woods and down an incline, shining the flashlight to light their way. He wished she would have let him carry her. He'd wanted to feel her fully in his arms again. To know that Sadie was safe and sound. He couldn't afford to let himself process through the emotions racing across his heart, but neither could he ignore them.

If he'd lost her tonight, he didn't know what he would do.

But why would he feel this all the way to his marrow? He'd lost Sadie a long time ago when she hadn't been interested in him. He'd moved on and let her go. They'd remained friends, sure, but nothing more. Still, no matter their relationship—friendship or romance—losing Sadie tonight would have crushed him. Before they exited the woods to find someone in law enforcement who could help escort them back—he wasn't even sure where—he stopped and drew her close again.

"Sadie, are you okay?" He brushed a strand of hair from her face, her skin soft against his fingers. "Did he hurt you?"

He held his breath, waiting for her answer.

Though her body trembled, she shook her head. "Not like that. No. He didn't get the chance. I'm fine. Thank you for saving me. I knew you would look for me and find me—that is, if you were able, but I just didn't know. When I saw the wreck, I wasn't sure what to do. I was afraid you were hurt and so I headed toward the vehicles. I wanted to call for help but my phone was in your car. I was so scared that you'd been hurt, Gage." She pressed her head against his chest and her shoulders moved up and down.

He held her, comforting her the only way he could. "I'm fine. I will probably have a few aches and pains tomorrow, but I'm more worried about you. And I want to kick myself for letting this happen."

She pulled away. "What? This wasn't your fault. Please don't blame yourself." She stepped back from him. "Gage, we have to get this guy. I wish I would have stayed and hit him in the head again, but he looked like he would get back up, so I ran toward the light and the shouts."

He allowed himself a half smile. Sadie was as

strong as anyone he'd ever met. "You did good. You have survival instincts."

"I think it's going to take more than that to endure this. We have to figure this out."

"We will." He took her hand. "Now, let's get you home."

"Where exactly is that?"

"I'm thinking you'd prefer to stay at your uncle Joe's with your family at least tonight. Am I right?"

"Yeah, I think that would make me feel better. But you're staying too."

"That's not necessary."

"Well, look, you don't have a car. Stay there and Uncle Joe can take you to the rental place. Please, let me help you."

"We'll see how it works out." He needed to contact Crowley about tonight and Thompkins to see what he'd learned about Sean's death. He wasn't sure how all of this tied into the drugs, but keeping Sadie safe was what mattered to him most. Staying by her side was the only way to do that. The only way to end it was to find her stalker and Karon's killer, and hopefully he would bring the maritime drug smuggling ring to an end in the process.

This guy—whoever he was—had proven he was determined to get to her. Did he know that she'd been with someone in law enforcement tonight? That he'd also attacked a CGIS special agent? Regardless, Gage had to protect her. His thoughts shifted to the moment as they stepped onto the road and headed to the remaining emergency vehicles, careful of the few passing cars maneuvering around the cleanup crew. He'd hesitated about staying at Joe's, but he was certain he couldn't leave Sadie alone and he didn't trust just anyone to protect her.

An hour later, he agreed to stay at her uncle Joe's. Sadie safely inside and chattering in the kitchen with her aunts Debby and Neta, Gage pulled Joe aside where they could speak in private on the porch. "I appreciate you opening up your home to me tonight, Joe."

"Of course. I wouldn't have it any other way." He scratched his jaw. "Though it makes me wonder…"

"Good. I'm glad you're tracking with me. I'm staying because I need to protect Sadie."

"It's that bad, is it?"

"Yes. Someone is trying to get to her. Someone tried to kill her on the boat."

"Do you have any idea why?"

"That's the trillion-dollar question."

"Do you think she knows something?"

"If she does, she doesn't realize it, but I intend to talk to her more tonight." What happened out there tonight was a close call. Even worse, it happened while on his watch.

"Joe?" Neta opened the screen door. "I'm sorry, I didn't mean to interrupt."

"You didn't," Gage said. "I think we're done here, aren't we, Joe?"

"Sure thing."

"I need to make a few calls." Gage eyed his smartphone after Joe went back inside. He called Crowley to let him know what had gone down, including that his vehicle was now totaled.

"Man, I'm sorry. Glad you're okay."

Gage squeezed the bridge of his nose. "What do you have on your end?"

"The fire chief says it was a gas leak that caused the explosion at the house."

"And we saw the guy leaving the house. He ran from us."

"Right. You and I both know that's circumstantial. But I'm with you. He wanted it to look like an accident, but now you're on to him. I'll contact the sheriff in Grays Harbor County and see if they apprehended him. This could be over tonight."

Except Gage doubted they had gotten their hands on this guy. He'd been slippery. He shook his head and contacted his CGIS counterpart, Thompkins, and filled him in on his day.

"Yours sounds more exciting than mine. But I did hear from the coroner."

"And?"

"Cause of death on Lieutenant Sean Miller was the gunshot wounds. No surprise there. He was on leave at the time, so no one in the Coast Guard had missed him. We've sent the two bullets to ballistics. We know they're the same kind of bullets used by the drug runners. But sounds like you have bigger issues."

Yeah, like making sure this guy doesn't hurt Sadie. Or kill her. But that wasn't his official job and he wouldn't say that to Thompkins.

"Listen, I'm sorry I didn't look deeper, dig deeper into Karon Casings's death. Crowley's initial investigation didn't come up with anything suspicious. There was no reason for me to question that."

"No need to apologize. We know she was murdered now."

"Right. Karon and Sean were seen together before she washed up dead, but she washed up two weeks before he did. He lived two weeks longer before he was shot and killed."

"What do you make of that?" Gage asked.

"It's hard to say. Maybe whoever killed him kept him alive and tried to get him to talk. About what, I don't know. Or maybe…it kills me to say it, but maybe Sean was involved with the smugglers and was angry about Karon's death. He confronted them, so they shot him."

And now someone wanted Sadie dead. Acid erupted in his throat. "It's all conjecture. We need to get our hands on the guy who's pursuing Sadie Strand and get some answers. He's our best shot at getting them now."

The screen door creaked. He was out of time.

"Gage?" Sadie's pleasant voice reached out to him.

"Anything else you need to tell me?" he asked of Thompkins.

"We're good," his CGIS counterpart said. "Stay alive tonight."

Right. He ended the call and tucked the cell in his pocket. "I'm done."

"Are you coming in?"

"How about we sit on the porch for a while and talk." Although that might not be the safest place. Still, he figured their guy was on the run. Who was he? Who was he working with? What did all this have to do with the drug runners?

Gage gestured at the swing and Sadie took a seat. He joined her. "There's something I haven't told you yet. A Coastie washed up on the beach and was discovered yesterday. His name is Sean Miller."

Her brows knitted. "You mentioned a Miller when you were talking to Deputy Crowley. That someone was investigating Miller. Is that who we're talking about?"

"Yes. We believe their deaths are connected. Did she ever mention Sean to you?"

"I knew she had been seeing someone. But she's dated different guys on and off. The last few months I have been seriously out of reach. I got an email here or there from her. I remember her mentioning a Sean in there somewhere." Sadie pressed her face in her hands. "I considered her to be my best friend—we'd been so close and understood each other. It wasn't practical to stay in touch every day even with today's technology because I traveled to remote areas in my research. But when I'd finally resurface and we'd talk, we'd catch up, and it was like I had never left. I feel like I should have stayed here in Coldwater Bay. If I had, maybe none of this would have happened. If I'd been a better friend, at the very least I'd know more about what's going on. What happened to her." Her grief-filled eyes searched his. "I'm sorry, Gage. I'm so sorry that I can't offer more help. If only I'd been a better friend, Karon might still be alive."

Quietly sobbing, she bent over, her hands covering her face once again.

Or, you might have died right along with her. But those words were best left unsaid.

Gage put his hand on her back, wishing he could take the pain away. Wishing there was something he could say to comfort her, but this was one of those moments when words simply weren't adequate. He wished they had met again under completely different circumstances.

When her soft crying finally subsided, she sat up and swiped at her red-rimmed eyes. Seeing her like this ripped at his heart. "Don't blame yourself, Sadie. If Karon was the friend you say, she wouldn't have wanted you to do that."

She nodded and sniffled. "I'm in pain, that's all. I can't make it go away, but at least I can try to focus my efforts on finding out what happened. Do you think her involvement with Sean Miller is what got her killed?"

"There are too many unknowns. But tomorrow, we'll meet with Shana and maybe find a connection. What we look for is a motive and opportunity. Who had enough motivation to kill two people and try to make that three. For my part, I'm looking into Karon's connection to the drug smugglers. The results of the water test might be important. It could somehow be related."

"I'm anxious to see the results too, especially if those results can tell us who is motivated to follow me and try to kill us both."

"Which brings me to this. Try to think, Sadie.

Try to remember. Is there anything you might know or have learned indirectly? Any reason this guy would want you dead?"

She shook her head vehemently. "Don't you think I would have told you by now? You know what I know. I woke up on a sinking boat. Do we know what they used to drug me?"

He shook his head. "Some drugs are hard to detect, especially if the lab doesn't know what to look for. I'm still waiting to hear back."

"I'm sorry I don't know anything else. It's all so fuzzy."

"It's okay. But please keep trying to think of something that might help, even if it doesn't pertain to what happened to you on the boat." Depending on the drug he used, she could have had an entire conversation with the guy and wouldn't remember it. But he didn't want to risk scaring her by bringing it up. Not until he knew something solid.

The thought of someone drugging her, leaving her to die like that, infuriated Gage.

"So you think that she was with Sean when she was killed? Were they on the boat together?"

"Could be, but I really don't have enough information to say." Which was beginning to grate on him.

"Well, we do know that I went to her home. I looked at her computer. Her mother was upset the sheriff's investigator thought it had been an accident. I think that whoever drugged me and left me to die thought I found something on her computer. We need to see if there's anything left on the hard drive. Some super techno geek could find it, if the blast didn't damage it too much. Unless he took the computer."

Gage had his doubt there could have been anything left. "If he wanted it to look like an accident, he would have left the computer. Just like leaving you on that boat drugged. Only you woke up too soon."

"I still can't figure out why he didn't just drown me and leave me on the boat."

Drowning had been sufficient to keep Karon quiet. "I'm curious about that, as well—if you waking up had been intended or accidental."

Sometimes criminals became overconfident. He'd thought perhaps this was personal in some way. Sadie waking up a few moments before she would die with no way out was some kind of payback. But the other pieces didn't fit.

Sadie leaned against his shoulder. Again, that supercharged current ran through him, through his entire body this time. His reaction to her wasn't anything new—in fact, it was a familiar sensation from the past—but it was completely wrong in this situation. This wasn't the time or the place, and especially not the woman. Still, his arm lifted and wrapped around her shoulder. His mind wasn't in charge now, and his heart made him a fool.

Sadie soaked up the comfort she found in Gage, the safety and security that poured off him. Now that she thought about it, he'd always been there for her in the past. He was there when a Coastie had broken her heart. He'd listened to her and helped her work through her grief. Heard her vow never to date a Coastie again. All of that seemed so ridiculous now in the face of this new life-and-death threat.

She might be shaking right now if Gage wasn't here. Or if someone else had been sent to protect Sadie, though she assumed Gage had assigned that task to himself, and that it wasn't official.

Unwilling to give up what Gage provided, she lingered next to him, leaning into him, his sturdy arm around her, for a good, long while.

Then she said, "Well, it's been a much too long day. I need to get inside and sleep. And so do you." She tried to shift away from him but he held his arm in place. He didn't let her go. When she lifted her gaze, his face was much too close.

Warmth infused her insides. Why had she never noticed her attraction to him? His broad shoulders, sun-bleached hair and those bright hazel eyes. His gentle touch and compassion. Or was it that she'd never been attracted to him like this before? Maybe it had everything to do with the fact that this man she'd considered no more than a friend had become her hero overnight. Protecting her, keeping her safe when she'd never needed any of that previously. Add to that, her attraction to him went much deeper than anything physical. Maybe that's because it had started with a deep friendship.

Did Sadie have it all wrong? Maybe it had everything to do with her needing his protection. The fact that he'd risked his own life to pull her from the water—and what she felt for him was only a temporary infatuation. Nothing deep and real and lasting.

But she had a feeling, a very strong feeling, that it could last. Worse, even if it didn't last, Sadie was almost prepared to throw her resolve to the wind and let it happen.

Except…

This was wrong. All wrong. She couldn't fall for him. Couldn't let herself be with him after all the heartache she'd been through. But as he dipped his head closer to hers, she floated. She knew he would kiss her. Her heart danced to a new song. Sadie had never wanted anything more in her life.

Her senses scrambled her head, so her better judgment was powerless to fight back.

The bushes stirred across the street. A dog barked. Gage stiffened, released her and jumped from the porch swing. Had his weapon out and ready to use.

Terror took the place of reckless joy and her pulse skyrocketed. "What is it?"

He pushed her behind him. "Get in the house."

"But Gage…" She was afraid for him.

"Please do as I ask. I'm going to make sure we haven't been followed here."

Sadie opened the screen door and closed it, but stood there watching.

"Close the door and lock it."

She didn't want to be away from him. Even these walls couldn't protect her like Gage could. But neither did she want to distract him so she closed the door and locked it. Through the windows, she watched Gage head across the street. When he didn't return after five minutes, she tugged her cell out, grateful Gage had retrieved it for her.

"What is it, hon?" Aunt Debby approached from behind.

"I don't know. Gage went to check on something." Or someone. *Oh, God, please don't let the killer follow us here.*

She hoped it wasn't already too late.

Was she putting more people she loved in danger by staying here?

"You probably need to go to bed after the day you've had. I'll watch for him." Her aunt had always been a nurturer, just like her brother, Sadie's conservationist father.

"No. I need to call 9-1-1." She eyed the smartphone to hit the numbers.

"There he is. Coming back across the street. It must have been nothing to worry about." Aunt Debby tugged the curtain wider. "You worry about him too much. That man can take care of himself. And—" she dropped the curtain "—he's a handsome guy, if you ask me. A good catch."

"I know what you're getting at, but I'm not fishing."

The next morning Sadie rode with Gage in a rental car he'd picked up earlier. She eyed her cell phone, wondering if she should contact Shana. "I hope we're not going to be late."

"We won't be." He steered up the road they'd driven last night.

When they passed the place where they'd engaged in car wars, the only evidence anything had happened was the tree Gage's vehicle had struck. A slight tremble started up her legs. She willed it away.

Reaching across the console that separated them, she touched his arm. "I'm so glad you're okay, Gage. You could have been killed last night."

Releasing the steering wheel, he pressed his left hand over hers on his arm and squeezed, but said nothing. When they parked at the agreed upon mom-and-pop meeting place and went inside, Shana wasn't there. Sadie followed Gage to a booth where they could watch out the window while they waited for her to arrive.

A half an hour later, Gage called her number on his cell and it went to voicemail. Finally, he paid for their coffee and stood.

"What are you doing?"

"Something must have happened."

"Do you think she's hurt? Should we call the police?"

"I'm not sure it's as serious as that. Something must have happened to prevent her from coming, that's all."

"But at the very least she could have texted you about that."

He didn't answer, but his serious expression told her he was worried.

Back in the vehicle, Gage started the ignition

and pulled out his cell. "I'll call her again. Text her too. See if she's okay."

But his cell rang before he made the call. He put it on speaker so Sadie could hear, as well.

"Gage Sessions speaking."

"Agent Sessions, this is Shana... I'm sorry I couldn't meet you like we planned. My boss gave me an assignment and he wanted answers by noon. I should have called earlier but I had hoped to get to our meeting." She spoke in low tones. "He's watching me too closely. So I decided to call."

Sadie shared a look with Gage. The woman sounded scared.

"But even though I can't meet you, I can give you the results of the water test."

"What are they?" Gage asked.

"The results are normal."

That news surprised Sadie and she spoke up. "Shana, this is Sadie. What was she testing?"

"An array of pharmaceuticals."

Well, that told them nothing at all...or did it? She studied Gage's reaction.

"Why would she test for that?" Gage asked. "It seems strange to me. There must be some reason."

"It's no secret pharmaceuticals have found their way into our water supply. Karon has been studying the impact of runoff pharmaceuticals on humans and marine animals. You know they get into the water through sewage. People flush their meds down the toilet. There's also farm runoff. It all goes into the water. I'm not sure why she came back to test the water at night while on her vacation. That's what seems strange to me, but I could be reading something more into it."

"And since the water reads normal it sounds like we all were," Gage said.

Still, Karon wouldn't have been testing water on her vacation. Wouldn't have done it covertly like Shana described without a reason. Karon was definitely on to something. But what?

Sadie leaned closer to the phone. "But when you say normal, you mean there are still traces of pharmaceuticals, just not in large amounts."

"Exactly."

"Is it possible for you to get me a list of everything that showed up?"

Gage glanced at her, surprise and admiration in his gaze.

"I'll see if I can send that to you. I have your card and email…" Shana hesitated. "There's… there's something else I need to tell you."

"We're listening." Gage set the smartphone on the console between them.

"I'm sorry I didn't mention it yesterday but I really couldn't. That's why I wanted to meet you somewhere else. Our boss, Mr. Epson, whom you met yesterday. He had a thing for Karon. But she didn't return that interest. She felt uncomfortable and awkward around him. He'd become jealous over a man Karon had met for lunch just the week before she left on her vacation. The fact that he'd known about her lunch, who she'd met, creeped Karon out. It creeps me out, as well. She felt like… Well, I should just say this. She felt like she had a stalker. And so she was secretly looking for a new job. Then she shows up to test water and the next thing I know… She's gone."

"And that didn't seem suspicious to you?" Sadie couldn't help herself.

Gage gave her a warning look.

"I admit it all sounds suspicious now that I've put it all together in one conversation. But her death had been ruled accidental and I guess I was shaken up over losing my friend. I'm sorry."

Gage shifted forward. "No need to apologize, Shana. You did all you could do. We appreciate you sharing all this information with us. Is there anything else you can think of you want to share?"

"Not at the moment."

"Well, you have my number so call me anytime if you think of something more that could help us. We'll look for that email with the detailed results of the water test."

Gage ended the call. He shifted in his seat to face Sadie. "Now, what do you think we should do next?"

"You're asking me?"

"You said you knew how to investigate." He grinned.

"There's no question we need to check into Epson's background. Also, find out what he was doing the day Karon was last seen. Her mother told me on the day before she was killed, Karon went to meet someone. Now I think that was Sean. Her mother was going to meet her at the beach rental house the next day but Karon wasn't there."

"I agree. We need to question Epson and find out where he was the day Karon went missing. But this, I'm doing on my own. I'm going to take you back to Joe's, where you'll be safe. If this is our guy, I refuse to put you in harm's way or antagonize him further."

Something about his tone warned her not to argue with him. That he might end up not allowing her to help him. She had to choose her battles carefully.

He started the car and headed back to Uncle Joe's.

When he dropped her off, he walked her to

the porch. "Stay here." He hesitated, then added, "I'll be back as soon as I can."

Sadie nodded, knowing she wouldn't argue with him. Had she imagined he'd hesitated because he didn't want to leave her? Well, she didn't want him to go. She didn't want to sit here and do nothing but wait. That would drive her crazy. She watched Gage drive away. At least she could research on the internet while she waited on him to return.

A couple hours later Donna Casings, Karon's mom, called Sadie.

"Donna. How are you?" Sadie knew the woman still grieved over her daughter's death, as did she.

"Oh, Sadie, I'm so glad to hear your voice. I heard what happened to you. I'm so sorry. This has something to do with Karon's death, I just know it. Do you have a few minutes to come see me?"

She'd have to borrow Uncle Joe's truck. It had just worked out that she'd left her own vehicle back at Aunt Debby's when they'd left the house for safety reasons. "Of course. Has something happened?"

"I'm not sure what it means but Karon sent me an email that you should see."

TEN

Uncle Joe steered his truck in front of Donna's house and stopped at the curb. Donna lived in Joshua, a small town on the bay side of the peninsula, but it took only a half hour to get there from her uncle's house.

"I would have thought someone from the sheriff's department would already be here." Joe shifted into Park.

"Me too." Sadie had let Donna know to call Deputy Crowley. Or she could call Gage, but Sadie could tell him when he got back.

Sadie got out of the truck. Joe followed. "I'm going too, so don't give me that look."

"Well, she might not want to talk in front of a stranger." Sadie tossed her uncle a teasing grin.

"Just tell her I'm your uncle. That should suffice. She'll understand somebody's got to protect you when your CGIS man isn't around."

The way he said that… "Now don't get any ideas. Gage and I aren't like that. And I don't need protecting." Sadie had traveled the world. Had gone into the middle of nowhere with fishermen—strangers—for her research. Still, she'd had a couple of deadly close calls, so she would welcome the extra protection.

Uncle Joe chuckled. "Right."

Sadie would have come back with something witty except as she approached the porch, the hairs on her neck stood on end. The door was half-open. She hiked slowly up the steps and drew near the door.

"Uncle Joe?"

"Right behind you."

"Donna?" Sadie gently pushed the door wider. "Donna, you here?"

Joe grabbed her arm and tugged her back. "Don't go in there, Sadie. Let me go in first."

"No. I don't want you to be in the middle of this."

"I'm already in the middle, but we'll both go in together, that is, if you think something's really wrong."

Sadie and Uncle Joe pushed the door wider to stand in the foyer.

"Donna!" Sadie called again.

Donna had known Sadie was on her way. Maybe she'd run an errand, except the fact the door was left opened like that seemed off. They continued through the living room.

Sadie approached the opening to the hall. A pair of shoes with the feet still in them rested on the floor, the rest hidden around the corner. Sadie's heart pounded.

"Donna!"

Sadie rushed around the corner to find Donna's form sprawled out on the floor. "No, no, no. Uncle Joe, call an ambulance."

She dropped on her knees next to Donna to check her pulse. "She's still breathing. She's still alive."

On his cell, Uncle Joe explained the situation to dispatch.

A noise erupted from the back of the house. Sadie's breath hitched.

Someone was still there. She slowly rose from where she'd crouched over Donna.

Wide-eyed, Joe ended his call, ignoring dispatch's request he stay on the line. "Don't you even think about it."

She snatched a lamp stand and removed the shade. "What? Are we just going to let him get away with this?"

Sadie took off searching the house with Joe on her heels. She gave him no choice except to follow. A window shattered. Sadie and Uncle Joe ran to the bedroom at the end of the hallway just in time to see a man wearing a mask jump out the window with something under his arm. He wore a black turtleneck and jeans.

Sadie would have followed but Joe yanked her away from the shard-laden window seal. "Are you crazy?"

Then he jumped out and took off. "Uncle Joe! You come back here."

Sadie wanted to go, but she wouldn't leave Donna alone. She was torn in two directions. But Uncle Joe could take care of himself. She hoped.

Lord, please keep him safe. If he gets hurt because of me, Lord, I don't know what I'll do.

She found her way back to Donna, who remained unconscious. What had he done to her? What had this monster done? And what had he taken? He'd been in the small office when he'd broken through the window. Had he taken Donna's computer? Yeah, it looked like it could have been a laptop he carried away, and Sadie could guess why. He wanted to destroy the evidence. How had he known about Karon's email in the first place? He'd obviously come to Donna's home to fetch the receiving computer. What an idiot!

Removing the hardware couldn't prevent a computer tech from finding the emails out in cyberspace, but maybe it could slow them down—maybe long enough the guy could destroy all the evidence. Sadie wasn't an expert.

It seemed their guy was getting desperate—only the guy who ran from Uncle Joe didn't have a limp. Could he have recovered that quickly?

Sadie called Gage but couldn't get through so left a voicemail about what was happening. He would be absolutely furious, she was sure, that she and Uncle Joe had left the house. Furious that the man had hurt someone else.

Though she couldn't remember what had happened during her abduction, she did remember one thing—the sensation that someone stood behind her.

And she had that same feeling now, that presence behind her.

She swung the lamp stand around to slam whoever was behind her in the head. He ducked and she missed.

He also wore a mask but had on a blue-collared shirt, so it couldn't be the same guy who'd fled with the computer circling back to the house. Regardless, she could only hold him off so long.

What happened to Uncle Joe? Why wasn't he back yet?

All these fearful thoughts raced through her mind at the same instant, but they were completely forgotten in the next moment when she saw what the man brandished.

A syringe...

Terror coursed through her veins. *Oh, no.* She absolutely couldn't let this happen to her again. "Who are you? What do you want? Why can't you leave us all alone?"

His mouth remained in a tight menacing grimace as he approached her. Was this the same man who had abducted her before? And if so, was he surprised to see her alive now? Then he would certainly make sure that she died this time. Or was it the man who'd tried to take her in the forest last night?

She would fight with everything in her. Die trying, if necessary. But she wouldn't let him take her and kill her. This man had to pay for his crimes.

"I don't know anything. I don't know what you want from me!" She swung the lamp stand again. But he ducked and almost snatched her by the waist with his much longer arms. "And who do you think you are hurting innocent people? Nobody even cares what crimes you have committed, so just leave us alone." Okay, maybe that wasn't completely true.

He seized the lamp stand and held on to it. She shoved it forward and pushed him away, then ran for her life. When she reached the front door, he snatched her by the hair and yanked her back. How many times would this happen? Pain rippled over her scalp. She screamed and tried to free herself, her mind refusing to give in. She absolutely couldn't let him inject her with that drug.

"No, please…" She hated begging. "I'll be still, I promise, just let go of my hair."

"Shh." The man whispered as though calming a timid puppy.

Definitely insane, this guy. He slowly released her hair and as he attempted to gently wrap his arms around her neck from behind, she turned to face him. He held the syringe between his fingers. The needle glistened.

"I promise," he whispered. "It won't hurt." A sickening, wicked half grin slid onto his face. He enjoyed this. "You'll love it."

"What…what is it?" *Keep him talking. Just keep him taking. Buy some time. Maybe someone will get here.*

"It's just for you. Something new and exotic." He gripped her arm and pressed toward her flesh.

That sixth sense he'd developed over the course of his career as an investigator kicked in as soon as he'd parked at the curb in front of Karon's mother's house. Something had gone terribly wrong inside. He'd pulled his weapon, but he had to be careful he didn't hurt Sadie, Joe or Donna.

When he'd received Sadie's voicemail he'd been furious but hadn't wasted a second heading to Donna's house while he tried to return Sadie's call. She didn't pick up. Joe either.

He ignored the fear that threatened to cloud his thoughts.

He didn't approach the house from the porch. Too noisy. He peered into the living room through a window.

The contents of his stomach curdled as what he saw sunk in. A man about to inject Sadie with something.

And she just stood there, unable to move.

"No!" He fired his weapon into the ground to warn the man off, at the same moment Sadie shoved her elbow into the man's throat. Gage sprinted around to the front of the house and burst through the door. Sadie slumped but he caught her.

"Are you okay? Did he inject you?"

She shook her head. "He ran off that way. Go get him. There are two of them. Uncle Joe chased one of them. Please, Gage, get them. And check on Uncle Joe."

He couldn't leave her again. Not after that close call. Sirens resounded in his ears.

She locked gazes with him and nodded. "Go, I need to wait here with Donna."

What had happened to Donna? What had the men done to her? Gage rushed from the house in pursuit, though he wasn't sure which way the guy had gone. He ran through the neighborhood searching. Caught sight of someone dashing around the corner a couple of houses down.

He sprinted after the man, adrenaline fueling his efforts. If he hadn't made it there in time, what would have happened? He couldn't think about it. That would reduce him to rubble.

Still, Sadie appeared to have been handling herself. But he doubted the man would have been so easily deterred had Gage not fired off a warning shot.

God, help me to catch him!

As he rounded the corner of a neighborhood house, he spotted a familiar man leaning against a privacy fence.

"Joe..." Gage slowed up and dropped next to the man. "Joe, are you okay?"

Joe gazed up, one eye swelling up pretty fast. "I think so. He coldcocked me. What was I thinking to chase after him?"

"Another man was in the house and almost took Sadie out." Gage offered his hand. "Let me help you up."

"No, you go find them."

"They're long gone. The sheriff's department is here now." Between the houses he could see the ambulance parked in front of Donna's home.

Joe let Gage help him to his feet, and Gage assisted him back to the house. "Let a medic look you over, okay, Joe? I don't want to have to worry about you too."

"You don't have to. Now go see to my niece."

Sadie walked alongside the gurney as they carried Donna out of the house and pushed the gurney up and into the ambulance. They wouldn't let her ride with the woman. Closed the doors and drove off. Sadie walked straight to Gage and she pressed her face against his chest. What was he supposed to do? Push her away?

Instead he wrapped his arms around her. Brushed his hand over her soft hair. Felt her shoulders rock and her body quiver as she grieved over Donna. Gage needed to find out what happened. Crowley spoke with Joe while a medic doctored his swollen eye. Gage was getting much too involved with Sadie, and he hoped Crowley didn't notice that. Or anyone else for that matter. His SAC might remove him from the investigation and give it to Thompkins, but then who would protect Sadie like Gage would? No one. Except Gage wasn't doing that great of a job, given the three close calls since Gage had been watching over her.

He slowly released her. He had to get a grip. Maybe she was better off far away from all this. Far away from him while he figured this out.

She swiped her eyes then lifted her gaze to him. "We have to figure out what was in that syringe. What did they drug me with before? We have to find out. Maybe this drug is connected to the water sample Karon was testing. That has to be it."

"It could help me figure out who else is involved in this and how it connects to my investigation."

Incredulity surged from her gaze. "Gage… you don't think…you don't think she was involved with the drug runners, do you? You're not investigating because you believe she was guilty of a crime, are you?"

"I didn't say that. She and Sean could have somehow gotten in their way and paid with their lives. I'm not thinking like a drug deal gone bad. Nothing like that. It appears Karon was looking into something on her own and got too close. On the other hand, their deaths could have nothing at all to do with it. Until I determine otherwise, I'm still here investigating her death. And… I'm trying to keep you safe. But if you don't stay in safe places like I ask, I can't do that, Sadie."

Sadie went over everything that had happened—as if Gage could forget. "Don't you see? It's a good thing Joe and I came here today. And Joe...well, he said since you weren't with me, he should go. But how could we have known this would happen?"

"I'm not blaming you. I'm more frustrated with myself."

She put her hand on his arm. He really wished she wouldn't do that, and yet, her touch was a comforting balm.

"I want to know how Donna is doing," Sadie said, softer now. "Do you think she'll make it?"

Deputy Crowley approached Gage. "Deputies are searching the neighborhood. Talking to people to see if we can get descriptions or license plates. We looked for the syringe Sadie told us about. Found nothing. Looks like they took her laptop, just like you thought, Sadie."

"How could they have known she was going to show me the email?"

He shrugged. "Maybe they bugged the phones. We can check into that. Which is just more confirmation that Karon had made a discovery and they were monitoring the situation. When Donna came across the email and called you, they acted on it."

Gage crossed his arms. "That email had to be no less than two weeks old. Why was Donna just now seeing it?"

"Maybe it had gone to spam or got lost and Donna found it," Sadie said.

Gage filled Crowley in on their conversation with Shana this morning, and then on his brief interview with Epson the day he and Sadie had gone to the office. "Since he wasn't at work today, I talked to human resources. They told me that he was gone the day Karon went missing. I'll have to track him down to question him."

"In the meantime, there's something I can do," Sadie said.

"I don't want you going anywhere or putting yourself in dang—"

"Just listen," she said. "We need to figure out Karon's email login. She could have had a web-based email server and we can find her emails that way. I wish we had thought of that sooner. Whatever she'd sent Donna is still out there in cyberspace. Unless these guys already figured it out and deleted it." Sadie shrugged. "They would have had to crack her password by now. Maybe they hadn't even thought of it considering they took the computer."

Gage looked at Crowley. "Or…in a matter of hours Crowley could have a judge issue a warrant. He could get a skilled cyber person with the right IP address to search for the emails. That only takes a few hours. What say you, Crowley?"

The man stared at him.

Gage lifted his hands. "I'm not sure the judge is going to buy my jurisdiction here. Sheriff Garrison can run this through. Or maybe the state police can do it for us."

Face reddening, Crowley frowned, not liking Gage's insinuation that he wasn't up to handling the more technical side of law enforcement. "I'll get on it."

And he pulled out his cell.

Gage crossed his arms again and glanced at Sadie. Gratitude reflected in her gaze. He hadn't done it for her. Or maybe he had.

"It's worth a try. And now it's a race against time." Sadie averted her gaze and stared at the ground. "I remembered something. That man, when he wanted to inject me, I asked him what was in the syringe. He said it was something I would enjoy. Something new."

Gage dropped his arms. "Say that again?"

"Exotic. Yes, that was it. He said, 'It's just for you. Something new and exotic.' That gives me the creeps." She rubbed her arms.

Gage's pulse ratcheted up.

A designer drug?

Illegal drugs could be modified so that technically, they were legal, that was, until the government got wind of them. Then they would go on Schedule I—the government's list of controlled substances and drugs that had no medical use in the US but could be abused.

Except what could designer drugs have to do with his maritime drug runners? They usually smuggled cocaine and heroin, and the maritime smuggling had increased over the last few years as the smugglers shifted from land routes through Mexico to the ocean. Pacific drug smuggling routes from Mexico, Asia and Russia were growing. The volume of drugs being smuggled was worth millions, even billions of dollars.

But designer drugs wouldn't necessarily be smuggled from those other countries. He'd contact the local DEA agent he knew and worked with frequently. See if he could help them identify the drug.

"Gage, do you think the drug he was about to inject me with was the one used before? We need to find out. Maybe it would help them treat Donna."

"Good idea." He pulled out his cell as he walked her to his rental vehicle. They waved to Joe, who got in his truck.

"What do you know about exotic drugs?" she asked.

"They're usually called designer drugs." Gage went on to explain what he knew about them.

"Are they dangerous? I mean, can they kill you like an overdose of cocaine?"

"It's my understanding that there is no guarantee how any one person will react to the drug—" Sadie couldn't remember a thing when she'd been drugged "—and they can definitely be deadly."

ELEVEN

They were back on the water again. Sadie stared out the window of the hotel room overlooking the Pacific while the radio played seventies music. She hadn't argued when Gage had wanted to move her again. To be safe, Uncle Joe decided to take Aunt Neta and Aunt Debby down to Eureka, California, to see the coast there. They had scattered to the four winds, almost. They hadn't gone as far away as they could, but they had still gone.

Everyone was scared.

Including her.

Arms folded, she leaned against the windowsill, letting the numbness take hold.

Gage sat at the desk with his laptop. Crowley had failed to get the required warrant to find the emails on the server. Gage was working off the possibility this was related to maritime drug smuggling and would probably have even less success than Crowley if he even tried, considering he'd need to produce evidence of jurisdiction. Crowley promised to get the state police working that end of it. But it wasn't likely the large company hosting the emails would so easily give them up. Getting their cooperation could take time.

It always took too much time.

In the interim, Sadie's life remained in danger.

So they were opening Karon's emails using the old-fashioned way of hacking her password. Gage could get berated for this, and who knew what else, but Sadie's life was at stake and he needed a break in this case. They needed to know what Karon had said to Donna in her email. Unless Donna woke up and told them, that information was lost to them.

"Any other ideas for passwords?"

"I'm fresh out." Sadie dropped her arms and joined him at the desk.

Gage's cell rang and he answered then turned on speakerphone. He pressed his finger against his lips to let her know to keep silent. "Crowley, what have you got?"

"Got the information back from the analysis on the dolphin pendant. It gave us nothing. Even if it did, it doesn't really tell us anything. Karon Casings could have been on the boat at any time. It could have been a convenient vessel on which to put Sadie. We're still looking for reports of any missing or stolen boats."

"It's too much to be a coincidence. But moving on... What else?"

"The vehicle you were in a collision with near the national forest—stolen."

"Of course."

"Donna is still in a coma. Doctors don't know why. They've looked for a drug but come up empty. You and Thompkins need to get with it. Do your jobs and get these drug runners. I have a whole county to manage. You're working one case."

Gage's jaw worked, and he drummed his fingers. Sadie wanted to say something in his defense, but she wasn't supposed to be listening in. "I'll contact Thompkins for news on the investigation into Sean Miller's death."

He ended the call then stared off into space while he rubbed his jaw.

Sadie snapped her fingers. "I've got it."

"What have you got?"

"An idea you can try for the password." She slapped her forehead. "I feel like such an idiot."

"So what's the password?"

"Trixi."

"Trixi, huh?"

"Yeah. Wait. Trixidolphin. Just Trixi isn't long enough. Deputy Crowley reminded me when he brought up the dolphin pendant. How could I have forgotten? That was the name of the dolphin at a sea life marina where she first fell in love with them when she was a kid."

Gage typed in the password and it opened Karon's email. "Yes!" He pumped his fist.

"Oh, no…" Sadie slumped as she viewed the email account. All of Karon's emails had been deleted. "I don't understand. I thought these guys were idiots, stealing the computers to delete emails when the emails could be retrieved from the server. But I guess they weren't idiots, after all."

"Don't lose hope. There could still be a way to get these emails even when they've been deleted. Someone will get that warrant. The issue remains the same—we don't have time to wait on the email. So it's a dead end for us. Moving right along…" He scraped his hand through his hair. "We should have heard from Shana by now. I should have seen that water report."

Gage checked his own email. "Nothing from Shana."

He called her again and got no answer. "Of course, she's not answering." His frustration came through loud and clear in his tone.

Sadie hated that they were getting nowhere. "Don't worry, we'll figure this out. I'll call her company's main number and ask for her that way."

He whacked the armrests and shoved from the chair.

"Gage, wait. There's a new email. It's from Shana. She must have seen your call, but for some reason couldn't answer."

He dropped back into the chair at the desk and pulled up the email. Opened the attachment. "Looks like she scanned in the results of the water Karon tested."

Sadie pulled a chair up to view the report. "Trace amounts of chemicals and drugs. This... doesn't help us."

"And I know why. Same reason they can't figure out what's going on with Donna. They have to know what they're looking for. Back at the house the guy told you it was something new and exotic. Remember I told you it's called a designer drug, if that's what he's talking about, and I think it is."

"So what's your point?"

"I'm calling someone in the DEA who is working the drug smugglers investigation from their side." He found the number on his cell and connected the call. Put it on speaker for Sadie.

"Finley."

"Agent Finley, this is Gage Sessions, CGIS."

"Sessions. How's the investigation going?"

Sadie wanted to ask the agent if he knew her brother, Quinn Strand. He was also DEA, but she hadn't talked to him in much too long. Still, she couldn't ask him because she wasn't supposed to be listening in. She wished Gage would just tell the guy.

Gage explained what they were coming up against. "What can you tell me?"

"Research chemicals. Legal highs. That is, until they're deemed illegal. We can't keep up with them. Unpredictable and dangerous as all get-out. You know the crazy ways that people have smuggled drugs. In bananas. Submarines. Avocados. Inside lollipops. Any way they can. Well, enter the online drug trade. It's a serious problem. With a simple click you can order your drugs online and they're delivered by mail to your door. Not smuggling them in banana skins. Makes it harder for us to get these people.

"We're not looking for a meth lab in a backroom kitchen laboratory. These drugs are often created in commercial labs by chemists. On the other hand, nonchemists can design them. Either way, they're black market chemists, if you will. The drugs usually look like a crystalline white powder."

"But can they be injected?" Gage asked.

Sadie realized Gage had asked that question for her benefit. He already knew the answer.

"Sure. As well as swallowed, snorted or smoked. But this makes me wonder how this is tied to the maritime drug runners. That's a different group altogether."

"That's what I'm trying to figure out. I also need to know the exact drug I'm dealing with here that put a woman in the hospital in a coma. How do I find out? The doctors at the hospital don't know what to look for or how to treat her."

"Considering there are hundreds of these drugs out there and more becoming available every day, that's understandable. We can send it to a lab to identify it once we get it, but that could take them too long to help the woman. I might know someone who can help, though. There's this guy. He's a clinical toxicologist. He specializes in novel psychoactive substances— another name for designer drugs—created by these black market chemists. He buys them on the internet. Tests them and gives them a name or identifies them and shares all the information with the authorities, who load them to a database. If we can get our hands on a sample and we can't identify it, then we can send it to him. He could tell us if it's made from another illegal drug and specifically what that drug is."

"But that's just it. We don't have our hands on it. Is there another way he can help?"

"I can't think of it yet, but I'll give him a call

and tell him what's going on. Maybe he is already testing something that could put a woman in a coma. Or leave someone with memory loss, which sounds more like Rohypnol—roofies or date rape drugs. That's a starting point."

"Maybe someone has changed the chemistry of Rohypnol then."

"That's something your doctors could possibly go on. This drug could be similar, only it's something stronger."

Sadie pointed at the computer screen, trying to signal to Gage about Karon's water test. His eyes widened in understanding.

"Oh, I might have something for you, after all. Karon Casings ran water tests that are suspect. I'll email you the results. Maybe there's something in there you can use. Or your toxicologist friend."

"Definitely send me those results. We need to get on top of this, Sessions. These guys are making me angry. And I don't like being angry. I'll do what I can on my end."

"I hear you. Feeling a lot of anger myself. Keep safe." Gage ended the call then stared at his computer. Blew out a breath.

This was beyond complicated.

Sadie moved back to the window. The waves washed up the beach, then slid back. She'd always loved the ocean. Wished for the carefree days before her best friend had been murdered. "I understand how that Finley guy feels. How you feel. I'm angry too. I'm furious, in fact. I think… I think Karon was on to something. She was digging into something really big and bad to do with this drug and that got her killed."

Gage stood. "I think you're right."

She sensed his presence right behind her. Much too close. His nearness and strength chipped away at her anger and frustration. Softened her up. Yeah, she definitely got mushy when she spent too much time with him. Gage could crush the protective barrier around her heart if she wasn't careful.

That old song by The Motels played over the radio. "Only the lonely…"

What in the world was she doing here at this moment in time and with this man? If only she'd noticed him years ago, what might have happened between them? But she hadn't.

That was then. This was now. And she couldn't let herself feel anything but friendship for him. Try telling that to her heart. Especially when the man stood right behind her. The melancholic song stirred her emotions even more. She had to break the mood before she did something pathetic and stupid.

"So what next?" The question came out in a

ragged whisper. Had she given herself away? Did he know how he made her feel? She hoped not because it could go absolutely nowhere.

He didn't answer. Instead he touched her arms, sending a current crawling over her and warmth thrumming in her belly. Then Gage turned her around to face him. At first she couldn't breathe, but forced herself. Except she drew in the scent of him. The essence of Gage. His gaze held hers and she couldn't possibly miss the longing in his bright hazel eyes. Deep, amazing eyes set in a handsome, trusting face. She wanted to get even closer. She wanted him to kiss her. She thought back to that moment when he might have kissed her on the porch swing, and she would have let him.

She would have let him kiss her! Her head screamed at her now, that she should step away from him, but she was pressed against the wall. And her heart told her to stay. She couldn't fight this—whatever it was between them—anyway, Coastie or not.

"Sadie." His gaze sparkled with humor. "Do I make you nervous?"

"Yes. Yes, you do." Part of her wanted to escape his uncomfortable and intoxicating proximity.

A grin cracked half his face. Her heart

flipped. She wanted him to kiss her. Wanted to feel his arms around her again. *Oh, Sadie, what are you doing?* Gage was as much a "victim" of their fierce attraction as she was.

One of them had to remain strong. Had to save them both. She had to try. Maybe she could change the subject. Get his focus back to his investigation, where it should be for the both of them. "So… Um…we have to get these guys. How are we going to find them? What are we going to do next?"

His expression slowly morphed from tenderness to fierce determination. Good, her tactic had worked, except she missed the tenderness. Had denied herself Gage's kiss. She wanted much more of him… Still, this was for the best.

Gage drew in a breath, their connection broken, and took a step back. Brows furrowed and eyes dark, he said, "We're going for a dive."

The utter surprise in her gaze almost made him laugh. But Gage chose to remain serious. He had to stay focused on solving this investigation and stop the drug runners no matter their venue, but Sadie continued to distract him at every turn through no fault of her own.

No. It was all on him.

But what could he do about it? He had to keep her close to keep her safe.

Come on, man, you can handle this. You have to.

Her life was more important than the struggles of his heart, than his attraction to her. And that was that. Gage would have to shove his personal wants and needs to the deepest part of the ocean and be done with it.

Her life was on the line.

But the way she stood framed by the ocean view behind her stirred his emotions again and reminded him of his near mistake last night.

He'd come so close to kissing her on the porch. What had he been thinking? He hadn't been thinking, and that was the problem. Hard enough to keep from falling for her when she wasn't interested in him, but now when she appeared to be fighting the strong attraction between them, maintaining control over his emotions was close to impossible. Impossible was one thing. Close to impossible, he could handle.

He had no choice.

"Why are we diving?" She'd inched farther away from him.

Didn't much change things. Her nearness still scrambled his brains. But it didn't matter. From now on, she was off-limits. He refocused on this investigation and his efforts to keep her safe and alive.

"The sinking boat you were put on could give us answers. We could learn who owned it."

"What if it was stolen like the SUV? Then what?"

"We could learn that too, and still question the owner." He nudged closer to her before he thought better of it. "You're up for a dive, aren't you? I know you're experienced."

"Sure. Of course I'm up for it. I think that's the best idea I've heard yet." She lifted her pretty chin high, purpose emanating from her blue eyes.

He'd never known anyone with more grit, more fortitude than Sadie Strand. He'd never known a more beautiful woman. Inside or out. He inwardly chided himself—be that as it may, he wasn't the guy for her. Nor would he ever be.

Stop it, Sessions. Get a grip!

His cell rang. Gage was grateful for the distraction. "Thompkins, I hope you have something for me."

"We've confirmed Sean Miller's link to our drug runners. Ballistics on the bullets we found in his body match the bullets fired at the *Kraken* a week ago when it got too close."

"Took you long enough."

"There's more." Thompkins sighed.

Gage tensed. "And what else did you find out?"

"He wasn't just at the wrong place at the

wrong time. I found evidence in his belongings. He was working *with* them. Warning them so they could avoid us. It sickens me to run across a Coastie working with the other side."

"Evidence. What evidence?"

"Cocaine. That enough for you?" Thompkins released an incredulous laugh.

"But that doesn't mean he was warning them."

"Doesn't it? Think about it. Sean was either a user or a dealer. The Changs are always one step ahead of you, as if they know your next move. We know they killed him. And if it wasn't Sean, then someone else is warning them about your every move."

Gage slumped onto the edge of the bed. "I sense a *but* in there."

"You're right. We linked him but we still don't know why he was killed. Karon was killed first—for all we know, Sean was the one to kill her—then Sean was shot and killed later. Maybe they held him for some reason. Or became suspicious or angry. Right now she is only linked by association and the fact witnesses confirmed seeing them together before their deaths. Unless you found something. Please tell me you have something more on her death."

Gage explained about the results of her water test and about his conversation with Finley regarding the designer drugs.

"Seems like she was on to something there. Maybe was digging too deep."

"I'd like to think it's that rather than she was involved with the drug runners."

"Maybe that's the connection—she met Sean. Went out with him, and he introduced her to his world or she saw something that made her concerned."

"Could he have drugged her and she figured it out? Took the water to test it?" Gage asked.

"That makes me even sicker. I wish he were still alive so I could get my hands on him."

"Not to mention that would also give us some answers," Gage said.

"Right." Thompkins cleared his throat. "Let's go through a possible theory on what we have right now. Sean was feeding the maritime drug runners information about the Coast Guard and where they were searching for them so they could avoid being caught, and maybe he was also involved in this designer drug scheme. Used them on Karon so she wouldn't remember her time with him. She became suspicious and started trying to find out more. Something happened and they were both killed. Anything else you can think of?"

"Finley is going to make some calls about what specific drug we're talking about, but we have to get our hands on it to know what it is. In the meantime, I'm going to dive this afternoon to look for the boat Sadie was on when she woke up. She believes Karon had been on that boat. Maybe there's still evidence. I'm only going to find and identify it. If I can, then we can send in other divers to collect evidence."

"Sounds like a good plan, but Gage, please…" Thompkins let his words trail off, then said, "Be careful. With Sean involved there could be others. You don't know who you can trust. So I'd hold your cards close. Maybe you should find that boat on your own if you get my meaning." Gage heard him loud and clear—he was advising them to keep their dive to themselves. "I have a feeling things are going to move fast the next few hours, which means our drug runners and murderers are going to get crazier and become more dangerous as they try to escape and we close in, or as they try to shut us down."

Spoken like a man who'd been through this before. Gage knew those words to be true. "And circle us like a great white shark."

Two hours later, Gage steered a rental boat— a nineteen-foot cruiser named *Sea Hag*—toward the coordinates where the fated boat had sunk and nearly taken Sadie with it. The North Pacific could be cold and brutal, but the sun shone bright today and the winds were out of the south between ten and fifteen knots. Part of the reason why he decided today was the day they should dive. See if they could find that boat.

The day he'd pulled her from the water had been rough, high seas, and the boat had already sunk too low for them to pull any identifiers, and then it had gone down completely. Lost to the sea.

And right now, he hoped they would also be lost to those pursuing them. At least out here he could be reasonably sure they were alone, but he would keep a sharp eye out regardless, Thompkins's warnings lingering at the front of his mind.

Be careful...

Sadie hung out with him at the helm, the wind trying to steal her hair from the clip. "Oh, look, Gage. A couple of whales. Slow up, will you?"

He decelerated and let the *Sea Hag* drift. "You're a marine biologist. Tell me what you know."

She quirked a grin at him, then studied the whales. "I know that sometimes it's not about scientific analysis, but just enjoying the moment."

"And this is one of those moments?"

She nodded, appearing completely content.

"It is." Then she laughed. "But since you asked and I'm a scientist, I can hardly let the question go unanswered. These are humpback whales, which make sense since we're farther out from shore. They breed and calve closer to Hawaii then make their way to the Gulf of Alaska in the summer. Closer in, we might see gray whales this time of year. They breed and calve off the coast of Mexico in the spring, and slowly make their way up to the Pacific Northwest for the summer. And that's the end of the science lesson for the day."

Sadie sighed, totally in her element. She looked like she could watch the whales all day. And Gage could watch *her* all day.

One of the whales breached—jumped out of the water—and landed with a huge splash, then slapped its pectoral fins on the water.

Sadie squealed in delight. "I can never get enough of that." She turned to him. "How about you?"

Sure, Gage loved the whales, but right now he was watching Sadie. "No. I never get enough."

He could barely see her beautiful eyes behind her shades, but she studied him. Did she have any clue that he'd been referring to her?

Any other time and he might have explored what was going on between them, but they were running out of time. She knew that too. "We need to get going."

Her smile flattened but she nodded, understanding.

He started the boat back up and refocused his attention on their task. Being here with her on the ocean reminded him how much he'd loved being on the water with her before. Spending time together walking on the beach. How hard he'd fallen in love with her. Twice. How heartbroken he'd been. He'd spent the time with her then, knowing she loved someone else. But he'd been foolish enough to believe he could make her forget her Coastie boyfriend.

He'd kissed her then. Oh, yeah. His kiss had been unwelcome and uninvited. She'd been visibly angry. Back then, he'd lied to himself. Told himself that she felt something for him but kept it hidden inside because Sadie was nothing if not loyal.

He'd made a fool of himself that day, and he thought he'd lost even her friendship.

Turned out her boyfriend wasn't so loyal to her, breaking their unspoken promise. And Gage had been there to comfort her. But a small part of his heart hoped she would turn to him. That's how ridiculously desperate he'd been. Her turning to him on the rebound would have been second best. But he hadn't had to worry. She didn't turn to him then, in that way.

Why, oh why, was he thinking about all this now? That was years ago. He had a world of life experience under his belt, and so did she. They were two different people now, and yet here they were drawn together investigating a murder. And he was drawn to her for the same old reasons. Only this time, she wasn't with someone else and unfortunately, she seemed to notice Gage. That shouldn't be a bad thing. In another time he would have rejoiced.

Except he'd sworn off loving anyone. And as for Sadie, he'd missed his chance with her.

"Being out here today. Seeing the whales reminds me of the dolphins and how much Karon loved them."

"I'm sorry." Yeah. See how it went? He'd been reminded of his time with Sadie years ago, and was she thinking about Gage? No, she was thinking about her friend, which is where her mind should be. Where his thoughts should be too.

Shaking her head, Sadie stared at the expansive Pacific Ocean ahead of them. "I still can't believe she's gone. Death comes to every one of us, yes, but it isn't supposed to happen like that. Not to Karon. She didn't deserve to die like that."

"We don't know for sure how she died. She could have been unconscious before she drowned. I hope she didn't suffer, but I agree with you. She didn't deserve to die this way. This should never have happened." A measure of guilt anchored in his gut. If he could have caught up with the Changs and shut them down much earlier, maybe Karon would still be alive. Except someone else would have sprung up to take their place. And if Karon was digging on her own regarding the designer drug, she'd unintentionally brought trouble on herself. For that he was truly sorry.

"At first I thought maybe Karon's boss had been jealous and this was all about revenge. But considering this mysterious drug and now Sean's involvement with your drug runners..." Sadie jerked her head to him. "Do you think her boss is involved in all that too?"

"No way of knowing, but I got a call while we were securing this rental boat. He had an alibi for the day she went missing. We'll come back to that if everything else is a dead end."

"And they thought they could bury me and whatever evidence I might have found by sinking me on that boat. Except I woke up. I keep coming back to that. I don't think I was supposed to wake up."

This part of the conversation disturbed him.

He didn't want to think about it. Didn't want to think about her sheer terror when she woke up to find herself sinking in the middle of a storm on the Pacific. Providence had brought them back together in that one pivotal, life-changing, life-saving moment. Gage didn't know what to think about that, except he was grateful Sadie was alive, and he had to keep her that way.

And someone else's life still hung in the balance.

Lord, please help Donna come out of that coma. Help us find the people responsible for this.

"I'm sorry it's taking me so long to figure it out," he said.

Hugging him, Sadie surprised him. "It's not your fault, Gage. Let's hope we learn something today."

While he savored her nearness, he couldn't forget he was spending time with Sadie now for an entirely different reason than years before. Today had nothing at all to do with his personal feelings. He wouldn't allow himself to fall for her again. Why did it have to be so hard?

She eased away from him and adjusted her sunglasses. He breathed a sigh of relief. And tried to shake the increasing feeling that they were being followed every step of the way, even out here in the water on this quiet, peaceful day. Would someone stir up trouble in the deep waters of the Pacific?

TWELVE

The *Sea Hag* anchored at the coordinates where the boat Sadie had woken up on had sunk. She and Gage donned dry suits for diving in the colder waters of the Pacific Northwest and prepared the diving equipment. They were here to see if they could locate the boat and find something to help them potentially identify the owner.

Gage had overseen the diving equipment at the rental place and now he double-checked the gases on their tanks, as did Sadie. This would be a deep dive. Not something for novices. Though she focused on assembling her equipment, she couldn't help but notice Gage's muscles in the form-fitting dry suit.

For not the first time she wondered why she hadn't noticed him before. His good looks and trim, athletic form were only a small fraction of why she was attracted to him. She couldn't explain it, but it must have to do with chemistry.

She couldn't forget that the man was a hero, her hero, and had saved and protected her on more than one occasion. Plus, he listened to her, really listened—taking her with him to investigate as much as possible, and letting her weigh in whatever they discovered. He was kindhearted and…wow…she was really making a list.

But she couldn't help it. Everything about him drew her in. But now wasn't the time for this. *Focus, Sadie, focus…*

"What are you frowning for?" Gage appeared ready to don his tank. "You're not nervous are you? We definitely don't want to go down there if you're having second thoughts. I figured since you're a marine biologist—"

"You figured right. I can dive, believe me. I'm not nervous, Gage. Relax. I just hope we can find the boat and get somewhere with this before someone else gets hurt."

He nodded, then his brows furrowed. He lowered his tank and grabbed his binoculars to search the horizon. His stance with the binoculars reminded her of a time when they had been whale watching on the coast.

Sadie had thought she was in love with a Coastie back then. But even though he knew that, Gage had kissed her. She'd been furious with him. She hadn't felt that way about him, but what a stupid girl she'd been not to have seen it then. Gage... He'd been in love with her. Was she deluding herself? No. He'd been there with her every minute, it seemed. Spent hours walking on the beach talking and laughing with her. Sharing dreams, while the man she loved was far away.

Why? Why else would someone do that? And that kiss—yeah, it had given her second thoughts, but Sadie wouldn't be unfaithful to her boyfriend. Except he'd found someone else while he was gone. Gage had been there to comfort her and reassure her through that miserable time. What an idiot she'd been. She should have paid more attention to Gage. And now... They couldn't go back. But when he'd kissed her, knowing that she was in love with someone else, that had effectively ended their friendship. Sure, he'd comforted her over her breakup. But afterward, she'd thought it best to distance herself from Gage and not lead him on. Let him believe she could never fall for him, even after her breakup. So she hadn't seen him again.

That is, until he'd pulled her from the ocean days ago. And look at her now. She was falling all right. How did she stop before she hit the bottom?

The last time she'd seen Gage had been the same summer she'd been interning at an environmental company, and she'd made a huge discovery that had propelled her forward into conservation. A chemical manufacturing plant had been illegally leaking pollutants into the river—a violation of the Clean Water Act. She'd received accolades for that accomplishment that couldn't have come at a better time. She'd needed the distraction. Her accomplishments landed her research grants and she took off traveling and focusing on marine biology conservation efforts, fixing the world one small step at time, as she always liked to think of it. Wow, time had flown. Years later, she'd been in the middle of research to secure another grant when she'd come back for Karon's funeral.

And run into Gage Sessions all over again. He said he didn't believe in coincidences. Neither did she.

Sadie hadn't realized she'd been staring at him until he lowered his binoculars.

His hazel eyes raked over her then back up to meet her gaze. "What are you looking at?"

"You." She wanted to ask him if he'd been in love with her before, but that was ridiculous. It didn't matter one way or the other. That was the past. They were here to find out who killed Karon and who kept trying to kill Sadie.

His face scrunched up. It was hard to tell in the sun, but had his cheeks turned red? He appeared unable to speak.

When he turned to search in the other direction, she watched with him. "What are you looking for?"

He handed them over and she peered through them.

"It's another boat. So what?" She handed them back.

Gage peered through them again, then finally said, "After years of experience in law enforcement, I've learned to trust my senses. That feeling in my gut. Regardless, even if I'm being paranoid, I'd rather be safe than take the risk."

"Are you saying you have a feeling the boat is coming for us?"

"Not just a feeling." He slowly lowered the binoculars again. "It's what's called a go-fast boat—hard to track by radar. That's why we've had such a hard time getting these guys. They're fast enough they can escape us if we do find them. They can only carry about a ton of illegal drugs at a time, instead of say, eight tons, so that's the only disadvantage to drug runners using these boats. But mostly, they have all the advantage."

A sick feeling roiled in her stomach. "I think I understand what you mean now about that feeling in your gut."

"I don't think they're running from someone, or are on a smuggling mission. This can't be a coincidence they're headed in our direction. I definitely think these guys are coming for us."

Quickly, they retrieved and secured the anchor. Gage started the ignition and steered back toward shore. Already the whir of the other boat's engine sounded closer, and it seemed to be picking up speed. "Yeah, I think you're right. They're headed straight for us."

Sadie's heart hammered.

Gage accelerated, the water hitting the *Sea Hag* and jarring them. "All this time I have been chasing them. The Coast Guard has been trying to track them down, and now they're going to chase me? I'm not exactly in a position to battle these guys, to arrest them and bring them in. Not with you here."

Sadie slumped to the floor, hiding away like some coward. She was afraid they would get her this time. They would get them both. "But we don't know anything. Why are they after us?"

"They're getting too bold and getting tangled up in their own web."

"But are they going to get caught or strangle themselves before they get to us? That's what I'd like to know."

He swerved the boat in a wide arc back and forth.

As a marine biologist logging many hours on the water—boating and scuba diving—Sadie never thought she would get seasick, but this set of circumstances was proving her wrong. She rose up, wanting to hang her head over the side during this high-speed boat chase, except the other boat was clearly faster. "Gage, what are we going to do? They're gaining on us."

A bullet pinged off the boat near her head.

"Get down!"

Gage returned fire and radioed for help. Clenching his jaw, ignoring the fear twisting his intestines, Gage accelerated and swerved to create large wakes to foil the faster boat's attempt to overtake them. More pings pounded the hull. Bullets whizzed past.

Too close!

One thing quickly became clear: these guys had no interest in overtaking them or boarding the *Sea Hag*. These were the drug runners he'd been after. The Changs or their associates. Were they after him and Sadie was caught in the middle? Or were they trying to extinguish them both for their efforts to crack the investigation into Karon's murder? He could sort that out later. He focused on getting them out of this alive.

But how? How, God? How do I get us out?

He returned fire and steered toward the coast. Help wouldn't come in time. This was all on him.

Pressed down behind the seat, Sadie covered her head and screamed. "Gage! Do something!"

But he was helpless! In all his years in law enforcement, he'd never found himself being pursued like this. Or protecting someone he cared about so deeply—he would do anything to save her.

"Should we surrender?" she called over the roar of the boat and automatic gunfire.

"No. Absolutely not."

"What do they want?"

They wanted Gage and Sadie dead. But she knew that. She was just panicking, and his own panic rose—bile in his throat.

Gage accelerated to the max until automatic weapons drove him to the floor with Sadie as the boat headed toward shore miles away. The onslaught of bullets took out the motor and the boat slowed until it drifted.

Her big blue fear-filled eyes looked to him for hope. He could read it there easily enough, but he had nothing to give. Disappointment surged in her gaze. He never expected to see that in her eyes. Never wanted to see it again.

Lord, we're going to die without some help here!

"Can we jump for it?"

"They'd only gun us down."

"They're tearing up the hull with their bullets. It's going to sink anyway." She put her head down, covered it with her hands and whimpered. "Oh, God, help us."

Gage could give Sadie a chance to escape. That was the only way.

She lifted her head. "I know what to do. Let's rig the boat so it explodes. We'll escape, but they'll think we're dead."

"You mean a gas explosion? That would be reckless and unpredictable and could get us both killed." He'd almost rather take his chances with these guys if they'd give them the chance. But they'd hit the motor and the boat was already slowing down as bullets ate up the hull.

"Got any other suggestions?" she asked.

"Nope." So that was it then. "So I guess that means we're going with your idea."

He didn't tell her but he'd had the same crazy, reckless idea. Sometimes crazy and reckless were the only choices a person had.

Still, she would be off the boat before he rigged it. He scrambled for a couple of flares and remembered the story about flare guns used to fend of pirates from the Somali coast. The flare landed on the pirate's boat and sank it. But that all depended on the boat, of course. He didn't expect them to be that fortunate or it to be that easy.

As for rigging the explosion, igniting the gasoline was the main problem.

Yeah. It was all a long shot, but it was all they had. That and prayer. Then they'd face their next challenge. He and Sadie would have to swim wide and deep then two miles back to shore and hope these men would think them dead.

Respect replaced the disappointment in her eyes. "If you think you're staying behind to ignite the gas, think again."

"Sadie, you're going to live through this. I'm going to set it off."

She shook her head. "Sure you are. But we'll be in the water when you do. Just pour the gas around, and through some of those bullet holes and along the side. We'll slip into the water and fire off the flare from a distance. While you're working, I can hold these guys off with your gun."

"We can't shoot the flare. Flares are not like bullets. We'll be floating in the ocean, with the constant up-and-down motion and aiming the flare for a ballistic arc so it would fall into the boat—pretty much impossible. Flares extinguish before they hit the water, so it could go out before it even hit the boat."

They were running out of time. They were about to lose this last option as it was. He was grateful they had already donned their dry suits, or the water would kill them just as fast.

He nodded. "So I'm holding them off. Pull the hose and pour the gas from the tank. See if you can drop our dive equipment into the ocean. Maybe we can retrieve it later. It's worth a shot."

"No. The oxygen tanks will make the explosion much bigger. But let's take the BC vests—buoyancy compensator devices—and the flippers."

"Good thinking." He nodded. That would help them float and also make better time swimming back to shore.

Gage positioned himself to keep firing at the men until he ran out of bullets. "I need to make the fuse," he said.

Then Sadie surprised him and suddenly shot a flare at the men's boat and caused a disturbance. He stared at her, admiration for her surging. Maybe the other boat would ignite and save them the trouble of destroying the *Sea Hag*, though she was already doomed. He tore a long strip from the shirt he'd removed earlier to don the dry suit and soaked it in gasoline. Then he would have to light it as they slipped into the ocean. Hopefully undetected.

Sadie shot off the next flare and received curses for her efforts.

Gage ignited the fuse, then he grabbed Sadie.

They grabbed the vests and flippers and slipped into the water, then swam a safe distance before putting on the vests and flippers. The seconds ticked by, taking far too much time.

At least the men still fired at the boat, getting their entertainment from shredding it, which also confirmed they believed Sadie and Gage were still on board the vessel. The men probably thought Sadie and Gage had finally taken bullets and died. They acted as though they would not be satisfied until the boat was completely demolished and went to rest at the bottom of the ocean.

"Now," he whispered. "Let's go." He sucked in a breath and he dove beneath the surface, pushed deep and kept swimming, Sadie at his side.

He turned on his back and above them, saw the flames of the explosion, then a second blast when the oxygen tanks blew up. Pieces of shattered boat sunk, but not too close, making him grateful they'd gotten a good distance.

He'd never wished he was dead until now.

God, please let them believe we're dead.

THIRTEEN

Chunks of debris rained down in the ocean from the blast, but none too near where Sadie and Gage swam beneath the surface to escape. They'd made it far enough away to be safe by the time the flames met the gas tanks. Lungs burning, she followed Gage. She thought she could outlast him, but maybe she was wrong. They swam long and hard underwater. Gage finally flipped around to face her then pointed up. Filled with relief, she nodded.

I don't know that I could hold my breath much longer.

Except he motioned for her to wait on him. Checking the surface for his drug runners?

Hurry!

Cautiously, he slowed just under the surface before he breached, then barely slipped his head above the water to search for their pursuers. Then finally he motioned for her to join him. She didn't take it slowly but burst through, wish-

ing she could breach like a whale. She dragged
in a long breath. She'd always loved the water,
but at the same time she feared death by drowning the most.

Treading water, she moved in a circle to get
oriented. The waves seemed choppier, rougher
now than when they'd been on the boat, and the
water was definitely cold.

"At least they're gone for now," Gage said.

"Do you think they believe we died in the
explosion?" Except now what? She and Gage
would swim all the way back to the coast?

"They must or they would still be hanging
around." He tried to hide his uncertainty but
she heard it all the same.

"They could also come back and check—we
have quite a swim ahead of us and they know
that will take us some time. So we'd better get
started."

The whir of a boat resounded. A measure of
hope surged, but quickly disappeared. The boat
didn't belong to the Coast Guard.

From a distance, they treaded water and
watched the drug runner's go-fast boat circle the
carnage—what remained of the *Sea Hag* floating on the surface, some of it still in flames.
They'd come back to check.

The men hadn't seen them yet. Maybe it
wasn't their day to die, after all. Except there

were still dangers ahead of them. She was a good swimmer, but admittedly, she wasn't in any condition to swim for two miles.

Gage tugged her down again under the surface. They swam deep and farther away, hoping to remain undetected. The salt water burned her eyes. She wished she had her mask. A snorkel would have been nice too. Might as well lament the fact they hadn't saved their tanks, but they could thank the oxygen tanks, and all the other accelerants and highly flammable fiberglass hull for the spectacular display that almost took them out with it.

Once again, Sadie followed Gage's lead to the surface. The drug runners had gone away again. Where had they gone the first time? Was there a bigger boat waiting somewhere?

Gage grinned. "We did it. We fooled them into thinking we're dead."

"Yay. A point for us. Maybe they think we're still alive but we're going to die anyway trying to make our way back to shore."

His grin dropped away. "Let's not waste time or energy then. We can do this. Let's inflate our BC vests. We'll float and swim on our backs as long as we can and then swim the rest of the way to shore. It isn't that far."

"Right. You're delusional." Sadie wasn't ready

to float or swim on her back. It wasn't that easy in the ocean with bigger waves lapping at her.

"Half the battle is in the mind, Sadie. Make that more than half. Tell yourself we're going to make it."

"And do a lot of praying."

"That goes without saying. God is with us. Never forget that."

After Sadie had inflated her vest and Gage did the same, he positioned himself on his back and started swimming east.

He'll never leave nor forsake you. She repeated the verse in her mind and heart. It became her mantra that fought the terror overwhelming her. With each lap of cold ocean water, she relived the trauma of nearly drowning only two days ago all over again. Her heart and spirits sank. This time she and Gage would both die.

No, that's not going to happen. You and Gage are going to survive this. I can do this. I have to do this.

She calmed her nerves and drove her morbid thoughts deep and buried them at the bottom of the ocean. Then she focused on one thing: surviving. A ray of hope shone in her thoughts and she reached for it. She wasn't sure she wanted to waste energy talking, but she needed to grip that hope.

"Aren't your Coast Guard buddies coming for us?" He'd made that radio call for help, after all.

When he didn't answer, she wasn't sure if he'd heard her. She needed to conserve her energy but believing someone would come for them would spur her on. Sadie had believed she was much stronger than this, but the seemingly endless attacks on her life were beating her down and dragging her under.

I am stronger than this.

But this time, somehow digging down deep and drawing on her inner strength wasn't working. Panic was close to setting in, and the last thing one should ever do was panic in the water.

"They're coming, Sadie. All we have to do is swim."

Right. Had he even been able to give their location before bullets prevented him? And even if he had, they would find the boat's wreckage and then search for bodies. Sadie couldn't listen to her own thoughts anymore. She had nothing good to say.

Her breaths came in short, shallow gasps. She wasn't going to make it, after all.

Gage stopped. "Let's rest for a bit. Just float."

And fight the current and waves. Easier said than done. "I don't get it. Why'd they seek us out like that to kill us? Don't they know that's going to bring a hoard of Coast Guard and law enforcement down on them?"

"As far as they know, we're dead. There's no one to witness what was done or who was responsible. That's why most crimes and violence that occur on the high seas go unpunished. The ocean is, for the most part, lawless. It's much too vast. Just like it has taken us time to find the connection between Karon and Sean and the drug runners. If we don't, then they could get away with murder. Again. If we don't survive to tell our story, then it will take them time to sort through what happened today and they might never know."

Sadie took in his words and let her breathing slow a bit. Her heart still pounded much too fast for comfort.

Finally, he said, "Are you ready to go?"

She nodded. They swam, letting their legs and flippers do most of the work, though it still exhausted them.

"Look, Sadie, we're close."

Spotting the small island infused her with hope and she swam for it, ignoring the burn and ache in her muscles, the scream of her lungs. She left Gage behind as she swam. Nah. He'd purposefully swum behind her so that he wouldn't leave *her* behind. She knew how he thought. The guy was in excellent physical condition. Sadie only imagined herself in shape.

As they neared the island, Gage caught up and swam next to her. "Be careful. The surf's getting rough. You could get caught up against those rocks."

"We'll swim around to the east side. Maybe it's sandy there."

"Right. We'll rest before we swim all the way in," Gage said between breaths.

Finally, he sounded like he was getting tired.

But swim all the way in? "What happened to the Coast Guard?"

"If you want to sit here and wait on them, be my guest."

"No need to snap." But she deserved it. "I can touch the bottom, Gage. Be careful of the rocks."

Sadie stood and carefully made her way to a gray sandy shore, the rocky outcroppings of the island protecting them from the wind. Then she dropped to her knees and rolled to her back onto the cold, gritty sand. It was better than the water. She'd always loved the ocean, but the events of this week brought her dangerously close to rethinking that.

Gage rested next to her on the sand. The waves crashed around them against the rocks, except on their small private beach where ocean water lapped up the sand before slipping back.

Up on her elbows she eyed the coast, gauging it at just under a mile. She wasn't sure where they were. They were far from Coldwater Bay, that's all she knew.

Gage propped up on his elbows. Arched a brow at her. "Don't think about how far it is. It's closer than you think. We can see it. It's just right there. We can make the next sea stack and then we'll be practically home."

"Not home, Gage. Land, yes, but not home. And those guys. They could come back and look for us here to make sure we didn't swim, couldn't they? Where are we, exactly?"

The whir of a boat motor resounded.

Gage stiffened, then scrambled to his feet.

Sadie's heart crashed against her rib cage.

Gage wished he had something to protect them with. He'd left his weapon behind in the frantic escape—he was out of ammunition anyway. He waited and listened to the motor, hoping he didn't recognize it as the one belonging to the drug runners, which would mean they had decided to circle back and double-check to make sure Gage and Sadie hadn't tried to swim back to shore.

He reached down and grabbed her hand, tugging her to her feet. "Let's hide behind the rocks until we know it isn't them."

"Oh, great. I was hoping you wouldn't say that."

They ran for cover, which wasn't all that much on this small island if anyone decided to do a thorough search, and dropped to the sand behind the rocks. A pang of desperation shot through him.

He was defenseless here. Helpless to save Sadie.

God, please let whoever it is help us. Sadie's exhausted. And I've done all I can to protect her and keep her safe. I'm at the end of my rope here.

He feared after the trauma of this week, she might have PTSD. He wasn't sure he wouldn't have it himself, even though he'd already been through hard experiences in his line of work. But never with someone whom he cared deeply about, and the difference was profound. But he couldn't let his emotions affect his ability to protect her, even in his moment of hopelessness. He pushed her behind him against the rock where they hid. Her soft, warm breath hit the back of his ear as they crouched low. Waited and listened.

"It's not them. It's not our pursuers." He released a breath, let his pulse slow and started to step out of hiding.

She pulled him back. "How can you be sure?"

"Wait here and I'll see who it is. It could be the help we need."

Gage left her there and jogged across the beach. Climbed over the rocks. He spotted a fisherman on his boat. Gage waved his hands in the air. "Hey! We need your help!"

The fisherman likely wouldn't hear them over the sound of his motor and the crashing ocean waves, but Gage would give it his all.

Sadie joined him, waving her hands and yelling. The fisherman jerked his head up to them. He steered his boat for the island.

"I think we're going to need to swim out to him," he said. "Too many rocks below the surface for his boat."

She groaned but joined him, hitting the water. Her slender form took off as if she was born to it, and Gage followed her. They reached the side of the boat and the fisherman assisted Sadie up and onto the deck. Gage too. He handed a towel to each of them. Gage eagerly wrapped it around himself, as did Sadie.

"Thanks for your help, friend." Gage shook the man's hand. "We lost our boat out there a couple of miles." He gestured to the west. "You might have seen an explosion."

The fisherman tugged off his white cap and ran a hand over his hair, then replaced it. "Didn't see anything. Don't tell me you had to swim to shore?"

"We tried and were resting on the island before we swam the rest of the way," Gage said. "You saved us from another twenty minutes or more of swimming, and I wasn't sure I had anything left to give."

Sadie eyed him then, surprise in her gaze. She didn't believe him. It was probably more that he wasn't sure *Sadie* was able to swim the rest of the way. He had much more endurance than she did, that was obvious.

"Do you have a phone we could use?" she asked.

Again the man shook his head. "I come out here to get away from everything and everyone."

"Your radio then," Gage said.

"I'm sorry. It's on the fritz. Been meaning to get it fixed. I'll take you back to the house. You can get warm inside and use the phone there. My name's Hank, by the way."

"I'm Special Agent Gage Sessions with CGIS, and this is Sadie Strand. We appreciate your help."

"No problem." The fisherman steered the

boat around the rocks and toward the shore, which gave rise to a cliff to the north.

"See, it all worked out," Gage said. "We're safe."

She nodded, but said nothing.

"Your lips aren't as blue as they were." Her lips. He wanted to kiss them and warm them up. Bring color back into them. He calmed his breathing and focused on Sadie's overall condition. "Are you okay?"

Dark circles framed her bright blue eyes. "As okay as I can be. Your lips…are…well…" Color infused her face. She grinned and looked away. "I'm just glad someone pulled us from the water. I never thought I'd say this, but I didn't want to face swimming the distance to shore. In all honesty, it might be a month before I ever want to get back in the water. And that's bad, really bad, for a marine biologist."

Gage wrapped an arm around her and she leaned against him, her form soft and warm. He could stay like this forever. "And getting in the water is a big part of what you do, I know. What you love. I'm sorry this happened. I shouldn't have taken you out on the boat today."

The Changs and their associates had just declared all-out war with the Coast Guard as far as Gage was concerned.

"You couldn't have known they would go this

far, these guys." She sat up, pulling away from him. "And because of what happened, we didn't get to dive and see what we could find on the boat I was on. They wanted to keep us from finding it, Gage. There's a reason. We have to go back out there."

"Not on your life." He wouldn't take her to that location again.

"You can't stop me from going myself."

"You keep talking like that and I'll put you in a safe house under lock and key. Don't push me on this. I kept you close all this time because... Because I knew you would investigate without me, and—" he couldn't prevent the flood of emotions, but he softened his voice "—I wanted to protect you. I don't know what I would do if something happened to you."

The way her expression softened nearly undid him. He gently tugged her closer and pressed his forehead against hers. He wouldn't kiss her. No. He would not fall for her again. But it didn't mean he couldn't care deeply about her.

"Gage." Her husky whisper wrapped around him.

If only he could show her what was in his heart, what had always been his heart. If only he could bury those feelings deep enough they wouldn't resurface. Regardless, he couldn't do this with her again.

"We're almost here, boys and girls." The fisherman's timing couldn't have been worse.

Or better.

FOURTEEN

He was going to kiss me...

Again, she'd wanted that kiss more than anything.

As loud as the warning sirens went off in her head, her heart didn't want Gage to release her. The gentle way he had pulled her up close and personal, pressed his forehead against hers, had cocooned her in sensations she'd never had before. Not with anyone.

I don't know what I would do if something happened to you.

His words and the deeper meaning behind them had pierced her heart, almost completely shattering her wall, and now that it was crumbling fast, she couldn't find the strength to rebuild it. Why would she want to rebuild a wall to keep someone like Gage out of her heart? Out of her life? How had a guy like him been in her life before and she'd paid no attention to him? Instead she'd let him get away.

When Hank had interrupted, Gage's expression had quickly shifted. The softness turned hard. The connection had been broken. Her heart could be left shattered just as easily too if she didn't remind herself why she needed that protective barrier.

He edged away from her, the lips that had almost kissed her forming a slight frown, then Gage stood. He helped Hank moor the fishing boat to a small private dock. Sadie took the opportunity to catch her breath after Gage's nearness. She sucked in the cool ocean breeze and let her heart calm. As soon as this was over and they caught the men involved in Karon's death, Sadie could distance herself from Gage. But right now she needed to stick close. She wanted his protection, sure, but more than that, she wanted to find Karon's killer.

If only being this close to Gage hadn't proven dangerous.

He turned his attention to her and held out his hand. "You ready?"

Sadie had to think about whether or not she wanted to feel the strength in his grip. "I'm ready." But she didn't take his hand.

A funny look came across his face at her small rejection but she ignored it and followed him out of the boat.

Hank led them along a path. "There's a stone

staircase cut in the cliff. I suspect you're exhausted from your experience, but I assume you're able to make the climb." He gave them a teasing grin. "Once we're there you can get warm by the fireplace. Use my phone to call friends. Whatever you need. Or I can take you somewhere."

"Thanks again for your help," Gage said, but he was looking at Sadie.

The fisherman started up the stairs and kept going.

"Are you okay?" Gage whispered the question.

"Of course. Why wouldn't I be?" She followed Gage up the steep staircase that would take them all the way to the top of the cliff. What if this guy hadn't come along? She would have been hard-pressed to make it the rest of the distance. And now she had to muster up enough energy to make the stone staircase.

Sadie kept up with Gage. She let anger and rage over what had happened fuel her, and she would have passed him on the staircase carved from the rocks had there been enough room.

This investigation had to end soon. They were getting close, but whoever was behind everything—the designer drugs distribution and the drug runners—knew that too, and given the previous attempts on her life and her pursuer's determination, he was obviously closing in on them too. A chill crawled over her and she glanced behind her at the view of the ocean.

She saw no one searching—not even the Coast Guard. Had they already come and gone, believing she and Gage were dead? At the last step, an old Victorian mansion that had seen better days came into view and reminded her of something from a gothic novel. She'd read her share of Phyllis Whitney and Victoria Holt novels, which could very well explain the chill that ran over her at that moment.

Hank kept plodding toward the house. He lived here? It seemed odd. Surely he didn't live in the place alone. She thought he would have mentioned his wife or kids or family by now, but maybe he was a private person and wasn't sure if he could trust them.

Inside the house, he led them to an expansive living area with a big fireplace. "You can have a seat on the sofa there and I'll get you some blankets and something warm to drink. Hot chocolate all right? Or would you prefer coffee?"

"Whatever's the easiest," Sadie said.

Though there was one chair, the man had said to sit on the sofa, which was more like a love seat.

"What? You scared to sit next to me?" That

same amusement she'd seen before shimmered in Gage's eyes.

"No. Why would I be scared?" She hurried to sit next to him, but the angle and size of the sofa made it impossible to sit far enough away so they weren't touching. Yeah, she was up close and personal now. "I thought you were going to make a call. I didn't see anyone searching for us, Gage. What's going on?"

"They'll find us. I'll ask for the phone as soon as we get something warm to drink. I'm worried about you. Your lips are still much too blue."

You could kiss them and warm them up...

Sadie shook off the thought. What was the matter with her?

"And look at you. You're shivering." He put his arm around her and tugged her close, rubbing her arms. "A dry suit will only keep us warm so long, so it's a good thing this guy came along when he did."

Hank appeared with more blankets and unfolded them. "Here, wrap that around you. I'll be right back."

Sadie took off the now-wet towel and wrapped the warm, dry blanket around her, as did Gage. Then he took another blanket and cocooned them both together in it.

"We need to get out of these suits and into some dry clothes," she said.

"The blankets will have to do for now."

While she waited on something warm to drink, she took in the setting. A few old antiques rested on the hearth. Swords above it. A shelf or two with books. The walls needed to be repaired and painted, but then she noticed another section that appeared to have been newly renovated. What was this guy's story? He didn't seem to go with the house, but what did she know. He probably inherited it anyway. If she'd inherited such a place, it might take her time to renovate it, as well. Time and money.

He returned with two large mugs and handed them off. "I hope you like hot chocolate," he said. "Tell me what you think?"

Sadie wrapped her hand around the warm mug. That felt good. She took a sip. Rich and thick and warm. "It's perfect. Thank you so much."

"I have my own secret recipe."

"We appreciate your generosity," Gage said. "If you wouldn't mind, I'd like to make that call. We'll get out of your way as soon as we can, and you can get back to fishing."

"Oh, no need to rush. I rarely have visitors here. No one to drink my hot chocolate." His tone shifted from hospitable to forlorn.

"I'm sorry to hear that." Sadie wanted to make conversation but was unsure where to start. "Your home is lovely. I don't mean to pry, but I assume someone would live here with you. It's so big. Do you have family?"

"I did have family, yes. But they died. At least you still have some family. Your aunt Debby is a gem."

Sadie froze. "I'm sorry, do I know you?"

Gage soaked up the warmth offered by the mug, but he tensed at the man's words. Then kept his calm veneer in place as he lifted the mug to his lips. He could better enjoy the hot chocolate if wariness hadn't churned in his gut since they'd entered the house. He could chalk it up to being anxious to get back out there and after the drug runners after what they had just pulled.

But that wasn't it.

Sadie pressed her hand on his and forced him to lower the mug, a warning in her eyes. Gage bristled.

In response to her question, Hank removed his cap. Gage got a better look at his pockmarked face. Debby had described the man who'd come asking about Sadie as having a pockmarked complexion. The caps on the hat rack in the hallway caught his attention, especially the red one.

The red cap—was it the same cap?

It had to be. The man had purposely given himself away by mentioning Debby.

This had to be the man he'd seen fleeing the house before it exploded. So much for him being just a nice old fisherman.

Sitting in the chair across from them, the man eyed Gage while he replied to Sadie. "We met a long time ago."

Gage remained calm on the outside and ready to pounce on the inside. He set the mug on the coffee table. How had he let this happen?

He was here in this house without a weapon. Or even a cell phone to make a call for backup. How had it come to this?

Careful, now...

He didn't want to set the man off so remained composed.

"I'm sorry, but I don't remember you," Sadie said. "Where did we meet?"

Gage could detect the slightest stilt to her tone—she was wary too.

Suddenly Sadie's hand shook and the mug crushed to the floor. "I feel... Weird." She reached for her forehead as she fell over on her side. Gage snatched her to him. "Sadie, what's wrong?"

She stared at him. She was conscious but in a daze. Her pupils were dilated. A tear leaked out her eye.

He lifted her in his arms and stood. "We're getting out of here."

"Not so fast." Hank pointed a gun at Gage.

Where had he kept that? Under his chair? No wonder he insisted they sit on the sofa.

"What have you done to her? She needs help." Had the man poisoned her to kill her? Gage had been an idiot.

"My special elixir in her mug wasn't meant to kill her. Yours on the other hand…" He gestured toward Gage's mug on the coffee table. "Was meant to kill. You've interfered too much already."

Gage stared at the mug, fear for Sadie curdling his insides.

"And you, Miss Strand—" his face scrunched up and turned red "—you don't remember me? How could you forget after everything you've done to me? That figures."

Hank glanced at Gage. "That's right. She can hear me but she can't respond. She won't remember a thing, which in this case is too bad, but I couldn't pass up this perfect opportunity to once again remind her. Now, sit on the sofa and put her down next to you." Hank fired his weapon into the floor, the sound hurting Gage's ears. Sadie scrunched her face and groaned, her head flopping back.

Anger burned in his gut as acid rose to his

throat. He couldn't take seeing her like this, and he'd been the one to lead her here. He did as the man asked, buying time, for what he couldn't be sure. But he had to find a way out of this without Sadie being harmed more than she already was. "Tell me she's going to be all right. Another woman is still in a coma. Another one is dead. So you're the one who drugged Sadie and left her on a boat to die. But you planned for her to wake up long enough to suffer."

"Nope. I didn't plan for that. A couple of idiots were supposed to drown her and leave her on the boat to sink. I already told her everything I wanted to say after I drugged her. She would hear and understand, but there was nothing she could do about it except know that she was going to die. The look on her face—it was everything I'd hoped for. Then I put her out completely so the boys could take her out and kill her. She was supposed to die out there and her cause of death, should her body be recovered, would be due to drowning."

"But they didn't kill her and she survived, and she can't remember. Who are you and what do you want with her? Why did you kill Karon?"

Calmly the man sat in his chair, still pointing his weapon at Gage. "If you're expecting maniacal laughter, I'm sorry you'll have to be disappointed."

Doesn't mean you're not crazy. Gage had to keep the man calm until help came.

God, please send help. Gage waited patiently for the man to tell the story he obviously wanted to tell again, so that Gage would know too, before they were both killed.

"I'll go ahead and tell you what I told her before, but then you'll have to drink the hot chocolate."

And die? No way. Gage would take his chances with the gun. "What's in the hot chocolate?"

"I already told you. A secret recipe. My own conception. I'm a chemist who is very angry—" he raised his voice on the last two words "—that she can't remember me."

He stood then. Started pacing. His behavior was becoming more erratic.

Not good. Gage cradled Sadie's head in his lap, her eyes wide and desperate with fear and yet, somehow the look on her face was peaceful. Uninhibited.

His gut churned even more.

God, help me protect her.

"My full name is Henry Snell III. Maybe that'll help you remember?" He spewed the angry words at Sadie. "Huh? Does it?" He laughed, and yeah, it was maniacal this time. "You can't respond to me. That's something I haven't been able to perfect yet. Everyone's response is different."

Gage tried to sit Sadie up and leaned her head back against the sofa. He knew she was getting this and comprehended. He hoped what Henry Snell III said was true and everyone's response was different, so maybe Sadie would snap out of this sooner than expected. Gage would do everything he could to give her the opportunity to escape.

"Wait. Are you—"

"My grandfather founded the Snell Manufacturing Company—manufacturing plastics, more recently, up to a decade ago, plastic water bottles for bottled water."

Oh. Man. Not good. Not good at all. The company that Sadie had discovered leaked pollution into the water.

FIFTEEN

Sadie hated this. She felt nauseous and woozy, and had no muscle control whatsoever. It was pure misery. And she hated having to listen to this man. Watch him spew spittle as he railed at her for not instantly recognizing him. For not remembering him. But she remembered now.

"You destroyed my life!" He waved the gun around. "Your little discovery that you *used* to make a *name* for yourself, a big career for yourself with all your special grants that let you travel the world—and, oh yes, I've been keeping up with you—your discovery destroyed the company. It cost us millions of dollars. The fines plus correcting the problem cost too much. My father filed bankruptcy and shut down the facility. He was fortunate he didn't have to serve jail time, and for what? All because a tank eroded and leaked chemicals into the river. That company had been in my family for generations."

Oh. Now. Sadie really wanted to be able to

rail right back at him at the harm his family had done to the environment and to the people in Coldwater Bay, who couldn't drink the water for months! She was glad she'd discovered the pollution leak. She didn't regret that for one minute.

"And do you know what happened next? My father died of a heart attack. The stress of losing everything, the very idea that he'd failed our family so completely, killed him. Mom followed a couple of years later. She died of a broken heart. That's a real thing. Did you know that? Maybe your time and energy would have been better spent studying that. And as for me? I was left as the sole heir of nothing but debt and shame."

The man yanked Sadie to her feet. Gage tried to stop him, but Hank pointed the weapon at Sadie's temple. "Don't make me do it. I'm not ready to kill her yet."

Sadie could stand on her own but her body wouldn't easily respond. She knew she couldn't fight him to save her life. He pressed his face near hers as though he would kiss her. In her peripheral vision, Gage tried to rush the man but the gun went to her throat.

"Okay, okay. I'm sitting down," Gage said. "Please don't hurt her."

The desperation in his voice could nearly break her heart. Yes, she understood people could die of a broken heart. She'd nearly done that herself years ago.

"Why shouldn't I hurt her? Oh, I see… You think you're going to be the hero here and then spend the rest of your life with her. You think you're going to be Sir Galahad saving maidens in distress, or rather this particular maiden. It's not happening." He pressed his cheek against hers as he continued, "I tried to move on. Even got married. Had a child. My wife left me because I couldn't find the job I needed to support my family. Who would hire me, a chemist who worked for the failed Snell Manufacturing? That made all the headlines? Nobody, that's who. So when my precious daughter, Kendra, got sick, her mother left us both. She couldn't watch her daughter die, she said. And that's exactly what happened. Maybe it was punishment somehow for the pollution, I don't know. But I couldn't afford the medical help she needed. All I could think of ever since that day was you, Sadie Strand. And how much I wanted to see you suffer and die. But how could I do that when you were halfway around the world with no real intentions of coming back?"

"What did Karon have to do with any of this?" Gage asked.

Oh, thank you, Gage. That was the question

Sadie wanted to ask but couldn't form the words on her lips.

I'm so sleepy...

Sadie couldn't stand anymore and almost dropped to the floor, but Hank yanked her to her feet so he could control her and threaten her with his gun.

"Karon could lead me to Sadie. I befriended her. Took her to lunch a few times. And like you, Sadie, she didn't recognize me. She'd already forgotten about the family her friend had destroyed. But more importantly, she gave me a lot of information in our conversations without even realizing it."

"Your chemistry concoctions, right?" Gage asked. Was he grinding his molars? Sadie thought she could hear that even from where she stood next to Hank.

"You could say that. But then she became suspicious. Started asking too many questions. And unfortunately she met a new guy. Someone with the Coast Guard—Sean Miller. So no more fun for me. I knew what she was up to. She was trying to make a name for herself like her friend here, and bring me down. I will not be taken down again by some do-gooder conservationist. Not when I just found my way back. I was able to keep this house, though most of the antiques are gone. But not all of them. And I started renovations. Things are only just beginning to look up. All because I used my talents, my gift to create something new. And unlike my father and his father before him, I diversified!" His face reddened.

"You mean designer drugs?"

"If that's what you want to call them, sure."

"What's the drug you put in our hot chocolate? What did you start with?"

"I doubt you know anything about chemistry so you wouldn't understand. And if you're thinking there's an antidote to help Sadie, you couldn't be more wrong. To be clear, the drugs I create are technically legal."

"Only because the authorities haven't discovered them yet." And only until the DEA added them to Schedule I.

"And that's why Karon had to die. She found out. Killing her would not only solve my problem, it would bring Sadie home." Hank actually clapped with the gun in his hand, showing just how off the deep end he'd gone. Had to be the drugs. And that terrified Sadie. This would make it twice now that he'd drugged her. Would she act like he was acting? Think crazy thoughts like him? Her mind was so fuzzy right now she wasn't sure…

She wanted to slump to the floor again, but he managed to hold her next to him.

"And Sean, did you kill him too?" Gage edged slightly closer with each question. Or was she seeing things?

"I didn't have to. He crossed the wrong people."

"The wrong people. You mean the maritime drug runners?"

"He and Karon should have minded their own business. They were digging too deep."

Wait a minute. Sadie turned her head and held Gage's gaze. She didn't think Hank noticed. Gage's eyes briefly flicked to hers, understanding in them. Good. He knew the quick-acting drug was slowly wearing off. Or was it?

"Digging too deep," Gage said. "I don't understand. I thought he was working with you? He was the connection between you and the drug runners."

"No." The man laughed. "You have it all wrong. And here I thought you were supposed to be some hotshot investigator."

"Do you even hear yourself? You've killed people."

Fury coursed through her veins. All she could do was listen. She was trapped in her body. Sadie wanted to scream. Who was working with Hank? They had to find out. She could only hope they would escape with the information when they did.

God, please help me to move. To do some-thing. Help us escape and get free. I'm so sorry for the hurt I caused him and his family, but I never intended any of that. I meant to save the environment and to prevent harm coming to those drinking the water.

"And Sadie? You said you wanted to kill her. You're the reason people have suffered and died. You went from a respectable businessman to a drug dealer. Aren't you ashamed?"

"There's more to it than that, but yes, in sim-ple terms, I fell from grace after I was forced into the drug trade." He ground out the last few words in Sadie's ear. She winced, moving her head slightly.

She tried her hand. Made a fist. Yes, the drug was slowly wearing off. She could fight back. But she didn't know—would she remember any of it? *Oh, God, please let me remember...*

She needed the drug to wear off. Hoped it would wear off soon. She needed to get away from Hank and over to Gage. Back into his arms, where she'd be safe and secure again. And maybe this time he would kiss her. If only to tell her goodbye because they couldn't be together. She had a feeling he knew that too. Suddenly all her strength faded and dizziness swept over her. Hank lowered her onto the chair, his dark eyes inches from hers. She closed her eyes to shut out the nightmare.

This couldn't be happening.

"I had no choice if I wanted to survive. I learned I could easily create new drugs. Legal. Perfectly legal. They're delivered via the US Postal Service." The man snickered. "Can you think of a better enterprise?"

Sadie kept her eyes closed as she listened to this man's story unfolding, hoping the waves of nausea would finally pass.

"Don't fool yourself. The changes you're making to illegal drugs don't really make them legal. They're not for human consumption. They kill people. Or leave them damaged." The floor creaked. Gage must be shifting closer. "Look, I'm sorry for your loss. All that you've suffered. But if your company was harming the environment and humans, then that had to come to an end. So you shouldn't blame others for your loss."

Sadie appreciated Gage trying to reason with Hank, but you couldn't reason with a madman, especially one who had let grief and bitterness eat away at him until he couldn't even see what he'd become. Until getting his revenge was all he could think about.

"But I don't care about any of that," Gage added. "I only care about her. What have you done to her? Look at her. You can't know what any of the drugs you create will do to someone. What if she falls into a coma like Karon's mom or dies? You have to help her."

Sadie peered up at the man standing above her.

"Help her?" A sick grin slipped onto Hank's face. He looked nothing like the "friendly fisherman" who'd rescued them from the island. He returned her gaze, fierce anger and murder in his crazy eyes. "I'm not a bad man. I wasn't a monster until you made me into this, Sadie Strand. And now that you're here in my home, I think I might like to keep you for a while. Everyone should think you're dead—lost out there to the ocean, so no one will ever look for you. Especially not here. So I can experiment on you with my new drugs. I need a guinea pig. I'm addicted to this new way of life. I think you'll soon find that you're addicted too."

Oh, God, please, no! Nausea rolled like waves inside her gut again.

"But you, Sir Galahad, I don't need." He pointed the weapon at Gage and fired.

Gunfire echoed in his ears as he dove behind the coffee table.

If Sadie's arm hadn't shot up to force the man's aim away, Gage would be dead. As it was, the bullet grazed him across the shoulder. Fire burned through him.

Ignoring the pain, he crawled around to get behind the sofa. Caught his breath.

Gage had anticipated where the conversation was heading, and that once the completely crazy man told him everything, he would then kill Gage. He'd tried to inch slowly closer so he could tackle the man.

The guy had obviously taken too many of his own drugs and fried his brain. Maybe he'd forgotten he wanted Gage to drink and experience death by hot chocolate, but no way would Gage comply.

Somehow, he had to get to Sadie. Get her to a hospital. Maybe once he knew what Hank had started with, the doctors could do something to help her in case there were lingering effects, despite Hank's claims there was no antidote. Still, she was moving now, so that was a good sign. Her pupils didn't appear to be dilated like before. She was coming out of it. But how much of it would she remember? He hoped none of it, honestly.

"If you don't come out, I'm going to kill your girlfriend."

Gage hated hiding behind the sofa like a coward. He had to give Sadie the chance to escape. He thought the man wanted to experiment with drugs on her, but he wouldn't remind the guy and push him further over the edge.

"Okay. I'm coming out."

Gage squeezed his eyes shut. Sucked in a breath. *God, if you're going to save me, now would be the time.*

Slowly he stood from the sofa, anticipating a bullet to the chest. He doubted this guy was a good enough shot to hit him in the head but really, what did Gage know. Nothing. Then his eyes locked on the swords above the fireplace.

"It doesn't seem appropriate to kill Sir Galahad with a gun, does it?" Gage asked. "How about a sword fight?"

Okay, this was absolutely absurd. But maybe in dealing with a crazy person, crazy ideas would work better. And a sword? Gage had no idea how to use the thing. He hoped the swords were merely decorations and that Hank wasn't practiced either.

"You can't be serious," the man said. He aimed the weapon at Gage.

And fired as Sadie tackled him. He missed again but kept firing. Gage ran behind a section of the wall but no farther. He couldn't leave Sadie. Depending on how many bullets remained, Hank would run out soon. But Gage had to survive the blitzkrieg until then.

He peeked around the wall.

Sadie knocked the gun from Hank's hand and it slid across the floor. Gage ran for it. Hank slammed her to the floor in his race for the gun. Gage beat him to it and aimed the weapon at the crazy chemist, noticing Sadie hadn't moved since the man had knocked her to the ground.

Hank laughed. "I'm all out of bullets anyway."

Gage aimed at the floor and fired. The chamber was empty. Still, he pocketed the weapon in case Hank had more ammo. And if he did, Gage would be the one to use it. But right now, Hank had no way of keeping them here, and Gage's priority was to get Sadie to safety. Call down the law on this house and Henry Snell III.

"Okay, so we're leaving now." He approached Sadie to lift her and take her out of this nightmare.

"No." Hank said, grabbing a knife from under the chair. "She's going nowhere, and neither are you."

In his peripheral vision, Gage caught sight of a big Asian vase. Was it an antique? He had no idea if it was valuable, and he didn't care. Hank lunged toward him with the knife, and Gage continued to retreat. He had to wait for the right moment.

Sadie groaned and Hank paused long enough to glance at her.

That was his big mistake.

With his left arm, Gage quickly lifted the vase and slammed it into the man's head. Dazed, Hank stumbled backward against the wall. Gage didn't wait to see if he would fall unconscious or slide to the floor. While Hank still held the knife, the man was lethal. Instead of coming for Gage again, he mumbled angrily and disappeared around the corner.

Now!

He had to get Sadie now. Hank could come back with another gun. And once he had her in his arms, Sir Galahad would escape with the woman he loved. Loved? Gage was done fighting on all fronts. He was done fighting his love for Sadie.

He leaned down to check on her. Maybe she had just bumped her head and her collapse had nothing to do with the drug. Her eyes fluttered open. Confusion rippled over her beautiful face. "Gage?"

He pressed his palm against her soft cheek. Her skin was cold. "We're getting out of here, but we have to be quick. Can you walk?"

When he tried to pull her to her feet, he could tell that the drug very much remained in her system, though before he thought it had been wearing off. Absolute fury rushed through him. What he wanted to do to the maniac behind these drugs—but not here, and not now. He had to get Sadie to safety and then he could come back with his backup and take this man and his lab down. He probably had a lab set up in the basement of this old house.

Gage scooped her into his arms and headed for the front door. He grabbed the big lion head doorknob and pulled. Nothing.

Then pushed.

The door had been locked. He tried to unlock it but it could only be unlocked with a key. Brilliant. He eyed it up and down. No way could he kick his way through that.

Time to escape was running out. Carrying Sadie, Gage ran in the opposite direction in search of an exit. He could break the windows and get out that way. Except…they had bars over them? Why hadn't he noticed that on their approach to the house?

He'd have to find another door then. He watched out for Hank in case he turned up again with another weapon.

God, please let the Coast Guard, let someone be searching for us. Help them find us! But Hank had been very much correct in that the authorities would likely believe Gage and Sadie had died out there in the explosion, and no one would ever search for them here in this old Victorian house on the cliffside if they didn't escape. It was something from a horror flick.

Gage couldn't let the disappointing thought slow him down. He would save them. He would rescue Sadie like he had before and see her look at him again like he was her hero. Adrenaline surged with the thought.

Breathing hard, he continued through the old house with its strange collage of gloomy rooms with peeling wallpaper and cobwebs, then found another door also locked that could only be unlocked with a key. But this one... Gage could break through.

He kicked it once. It didn't budge. This was going to take more effort.

He gently set Sadie down. "It's going to be okay. I'm going to get us out of this."

Her smile was dreamy. "Thanks."

"If you can please keep an eye out for Hank. Warn me if you see him coming."

"Okay."

He wasn't sure he could count on her for that kind of assistance, but on the other hand, she'd saved his life twice today already. The least he could do was return the favor.

He scanned the long hallway. Maybe there was another display of weapons on the wall. An ax would be nice. He could chop his way through that door. And as for a phone, he hadn't seen one yet. Likely the only communication was Hank's cell phone.

Gage kicked the door. The noise would unfortunately draw Hank's attention, but it couldn't be helped. Where had that man run off to anyway?

He kicked again and again until finally the door splintered and Gage opened it all the way. He lifted Sadie back into his arms and went through the door and found himself in the backyard of the house. Sadie in his arms, he trudged around the house, keeping a distance and an eye out in case Hank appeared in a window and tried to shoot them. Gage found no vehicle in which they could escape, and he couldn't keep carrying her like this. He had to take a break, but he didn't want to risk it. He had to keep moving until they were a safe distance away.

"The boat," she said. "And Gage—" she pressed her hand against his chest "—you can put me down now."

He didn't want to release her. In his arms, her soft form pressed against him, her face was near and her big beautiful blue eyes gazed into his. An emotion he wouldn't even attempt to describe lingered there. Her lips drew him in. He sucked in a breath and regained his composure—this wasn't the time to kiss her. Wasn't the time? As if there *ever would* be a time to kiss her? What happened to his resolve?

"Are you sure you're okay?" he asked.

She nodded. "Yes. A little shaky maybe, but you can't keep going like this."

Gently he set her on her feet.

"Let's take the stone steps," she said. "We can use his boat and go down the coast until we find a town and can call for help. Or… Maybe your Coast Guard buddies will show up."

Right. "Go ahead and joke about it."

He took her hand and they jogged around the house, keeping to the trees and shadows until they made it to the front. They'd have to sneak across to the stairs. But where had he gone? Was he watching for them, waiting to shoot them down as they made their escape? The property was secluded. Nobody would know or care if he shot them.

They ran toward the staircase without anyone standing in their way. At the top of the steps, Gage studied their long hike down. One misstep on these steep and winding stairs could be deadly.

"Are you sure you're okay to do this?" he asked.

Though the look in her eyes told him she was uncertain, she nodded.

"I'll go first," he said. "Let's hold hands."

That way if she tripped or collapsed, he could catch her. He hoped.

Carefully they descended the steps. In the distance he searched for the help that never came. Wasn't ever going to come.

They hit a switchback in the staircase and Gage stepped around the corner.

Henry Snell III pointed a gun at them.

SIXTEEN

Sadie jumped at the sight of him. She wanted to push the man down the staircase and be done with this. "How did you beat us?"

"There's this tunnel from the house, see?" He gestured to his right. "You have to know where to look. I'm going to need you to follow me back into the house now. I like my privacy, and out in the open like this, we're a little too visible."

"There's nobody around to see," she said.

"Sadie." Gage squeezed her hand. "Just do as the man says."

Right. She was being an idiot. They needed to buy themselves time. She squeezed his hand back, letting him know she would comply. But they needed to get out of this. She groped a rock next to her and tucked it under her arm as she followed Gage into the dark tunnel that led back to the house. Of course there would be a hidden passage. This old Victorian mansion had probably actually appeared in a gothic novel somewhere.

Hank jabbed the muzzle into her back. "I much prefer using the drugs to get compliance. Hate using guns. But I will use it if you make me."

The dark tunnel twisted and turned and inclined without steps. Her breaths came hard and fast along with her increased heart rate, and sweat beaded on her face—she thought it was more than she should experience with the physical exertion. A side effect of the drug?

She really wanted to punch the guy for doing this to her. For killing Karon.

Come on, Gage. Do something!

But she knew he wouldn't even try until he knew he could do it without Sadie getting hurt.

"Ouch!" Sadie bent over to examine her ankle.

Hank stumbled closer to her. She rose to her full height and swung the rock around, hoping to connect with his temple, but he was faster than her and gripped her wrist. She struggled with him. Gage rushed forward.

"No, Gage!" she screamed and kicked the gun up as it fired off. She was getting good at redirecting Hank's bullets meant for Gage.

How many times would she have to do this? Still, Gage had taken the chance she'd given him. He slammed the man into the wall. The gun fired off again. Now that Sadie was free from his grip, she searched for her rock. She could hit him again.

"Run, Sadie. Go get help!" Gage yelled. "Get out of here."

Hank landed a punch at Gage. Held the gun up but it misfired. Gage wrestled the weapon from him and tossed it away. Sadie grabbed it.

"No, Sadie. If it misfires, it can't be trusted. It could hurt you. It's no use to us."

Hank punched Gage in the face. He returned the favor and the fighting began. To Sadie, it looked like Hank was a skilled fighter even without his sword, preventing Gage from easily taking him down and out, weapon or not.

Sadie wasn't sure which of them would win this fight. She had to do something. Grunting and groaning, the two men fought and tumbled out onto the stone steps. She followed them out of the tunnel. A gust of salty breeze knocked into her. Dizziness swept over her again.

But she didn't have time to think about herself or care. Hank had thrown multiple punches at Gage. He wasn't fighting back anymore.

Oh, God, please, help Gage!

"Gage, come on, get up!"

Suddenly Gage rolled out of Hank's way.

With nothing to receive his punch but air, Hank stumbled forward and he fell over the side.

Gage and Sadie ran to the edge. Hank held on to the stone ledge. "Help me! I'm going to fall. You can't let me fall."

Gage reached for the man, his hands bloodied and slippery. Henry Snell III's eyes filled with tears and a clarity she hadn't seen in them before. "I'm a monster. What have I become? I let everything in life beat me down and bring me to…to what…to this? To die on the rocks at the bottom of a cliff?"

Sadie leaned down to help.

"Get back," Gage said. "You can't reach him anyway."

She held on to Gage's waist as he leaned farther, reaching, stretching. He groaned. "Hold on!"

But he wasn't talking to Sadie—he was talking to Hank.

Guilt suffused her. She couldn't find it in herself to hope he made it, after everything he'd put them through. *God, forgive me! Please… Help us to help him.*

"You can let go now, Sadie," Gage said. "I promise. I'm not going to slip over with Hank."

She wasn't so sure that was true, but she edged away and looked Hank in the eyes again—that he was a man fighting for his life, clinging to a lifeline, was written all over his face. She wanted to feel sorry for him. A lump formed in her throat.

Then she remembered. He'd mentioned that Sean had crossed someone. This whole time and they believed Sean had gotten involved with drug runners and it was a drug deal gone bad. "Tell us… Who were you working with? Who killed Sean?"

"What?" He seemed to dig deep and find some kind of resolve. He would live, after all. Live another day to try and kill her and Gage. "I'll tell you once you bring me up."

Suddenly his hands slipped free of Gage's and he tumbled away.

Shock surged through Gage as he watched the man fall. Hank's eyes widened with terror as he stared back at Gage. Still believing he could somehow survive, grasping at the hope of living, while his body plummeted nearly a hundred feet. His mind would never comprehend the reality of his imminent death before he died.

The man hit the rocks, his screams silenced.

But Gage could still hear those screams. He could still see those haunted eyes.

Stunned, Gage remained looking on. Waves crashed against the rocks and over Hank's body like he already belonged to the ocean. Soon they would carry him away.

Gage needed to find a phone. Let the authorities know where they were and get someone to retrieve Hank's body before the ocean carried it away, if possible. He pulled his gaze from the sight to focus on Sadie. She'd whipped her head around to avoid the gruesome scene, and for that he was grateful. Her eyes were still squeezed shut.

"Come here." He gently took her in his arms and smoothed her silky hair with his hand.

"Is it over?"

At least this part of it was over. But there was still someone out there, if Hank could be believed, who had killed Sean. Someone who had given away Gage's location today—and only one other person knew where they were headed.

They had been led to believe that Sean had been the inside man, working with the maritime drug runners and the designer drug distribution, as well. The possibilities of just who was playing both sides sent cold chills all over Gage. At least for now, Sadie had been spared.

He pushed past the knot in his throat. "I wish I could tell you yes…"

"But it's not over yet." Her voice shook.

"Not until we find everyone involved." He held

her closer, tighter against him. He never wanted to let her go. "Let's get you somewhere safe."

She sagged against him. "Safe. I have no idea where that would be. Do you?"

He thought she would be safest with him, but everything that happened said differently. "A safe house maybe, just until this is over." He released her and gripped her arms, forcing her to look at him. "But you can't leave or try to investigate on your own this time. Do you understand?"

She stared at him, unwilling to answer him.

He gently shook her. "Sadie, you have almost died I don't know how many times. I'm this close—" he held his fingers close together "—to finding who is responsible. Let me do my job without having to worry about protecting you."

"I never asked you to protect me. You insisted I stick close to you."

Was she actually trying to blame this on him? Maybe she was right. He could almost feel the sting against his cheek as if she'd slapped him. He released her, letting the cold reality knock sense into him. He had to disconnect from her emotionally. And one way or another, he would. "Let's go find a phone."

He turned and started hiking toward the tunnel.

"Gage, wait."

He was done waiting. Done letting the crazy way she made him feel control his every action. He couldn't be her protector anymore. He had never been the right person to protect her.

"Gage!" She grabbed his arm and tried to pull him to face her. "Wait. I'm… I'm sorry for what I said. Without you, I'd be dead already. I'm just tired and scared and—"

"Sadie!" She'd collapsed, but he caught her. "The drugs are still messing with you."

She rolled her head back and around to lean against him. "Yes. I feel dizzy and nauseous."

He had to get her to a hospital. He rushed through the tunnel with her in his arms again. It seemed a safer path than the steep stone staircase. He just hoped it would take him where he needed to go and find Hank's cell or another way to communicate. Otherwise, he'd have to carry her back down and take the boat like she'd suggested.

He ran with her in his arms, his breaths coming faster.

"Let me walk, Gage. I'm okay now."

"Are you sure?"

She nodded. "I want to walk or run. We need to hurry."

He slowed and set her down. Brushed his hand through her hair. "Let me know if you feel dizzy again."

"I will. I promise."

Gage grabbed her hand and together they continued through the tunnel.

Voices up ahead grew louder.

He stopped and edged back. Friend or foe?

He had the gut feeling they weren't friendly. But even if he didn't, they couldn't take the risk and just step out and identify themselves.

SEVENTEEN

Gage's frown deepened. He grabbed her hand and led her back the way they came. She knew better than to even ask him a question. They had to keep quiet because their voices would carry and alert the men they were in the tunnel. Gage had taken Hank's new gun but since it had misfired, it worked no better than the previous gun. Unless he could use it to bluff his way. It would likely be a last resort.

These guys were either the guys in that go-fast boat or the two that came to Donna's house and had drugged Donna and tried to drug Sadie. Just how many people could be involved in drug trafficking, no matter the channels? Regardless, she didn't want to face them.

And Sadie had absolutely no intention of being taken by one of these men again. Drugged again so that she would either die or she couldn't remember later what had happened.

She ran behind Gage, but the strange sweating started up again. Dizziness tried to take ahold of her. She had to keep going, but it was like running up against a brick wall. Her body would not cooperate. She stumbled forward and would have hit the ground, but Gage scooped her up without a word.

She was so grateful to him.

Outside the ocean breeze wrapped around her. "I'm going to sit you here on the steps. Hide behind this rock if you can, and I'm going back inside to face them."

"No," she whispered. "You can't. Just take me down to the boat. We'll escape that way."

"There's no time. We'd never make it if they have guns, and it's likely they do. Now wait here. Trust me on this. I have a plan."

He disappeared back into the tunnel. "Gage... wait..."

Don't go!

Unarmed, how could he hope to take on those men? Sadie wasn't about to let him do that alone. Finding a rock she could use as a weapon, she headed back into the tunnel and searched for a place to hide in case Gage needed her. She could use the element of surprise. She didn't have a flashlight. Gage had taken that, but light filtered in from the exit, growing dimmer the deeper she went.

A hand clamped over her mouth. Sadie tried

to use the rock, but he tightened his grip and whispered in her ear. "I told you to stay put. What are you doing?"

He released her and pulled her into a shadowed groove.

She stood on her toes and whispered into his ear. "I'm hiding with you. I brought a weapon."

A tenuous grin slid into his face, then he positioned her behind him.

The men were almost upon them. Sadie was more than glad that Gage had caught her and pulled her into the shadows. The men seemed oblivious to their partner's demise—or had he been their boss? Still, there was someone else involved. Someone they hadn't figured on.

Sadie stood behind Gage and held her breath. Her hand pressed against his back; she could feel when his muscles tensed. The men walked past them in the shadows. Gage lunged at one and kicked the other. He wrestled the weapon from his holster. The other man charged Gage, but Sadie slammed him in the head with the rock, knocking him nearly unconscious. She straddled him, searching for his weapons. Found a knife and a gun.

And she recognized his dazed eyes as he stared up at her. He was the man who'd been at Donna's house and tried to inject her with that drug. And now she realized, he'd been on the boat that had shot the *Sea Hag* to pieces.

Confusion shifted to recognition and his eyes grew wide. *Uh-oh.* She'd waited too long. Before she could react, he grabbed her by the wrist. Behind her, she heard punches and kicks. Groans and shouts. Sadie fought and twisted enough to aim the gun and shot it next to his head. The man instantly let go. She jumped from him and pointed the weapon at the man Gage fought. Gage gained control and pointed a weapon at the man too.

"Lee and Charles Chang, you're both under arrest for maritime drug smuggling, fleeing the Coast Guard, murder and attempted murder."

"You don't have any proof." The shorter guy spat at Gage. "You got nothing on us."

"I have all the proof I need. You two fired on us today. Tried to sink our boat and kill us."

"You have the wrong guys. We don't know nothing, man. We were just using this tunnel."

"Right. Using this tunnel to smuggle drugs. And you're going straight to prison. Now I want to know who else is involved."

"We're not smuggling drugs. No one else is involved."

That sounded kind of contradictory to Sadie.

"Look, you can't arrest us," the man on the ground said. He finally scrambled to his feet, but Sadie now aimed her weapon at him. "He's going to kill us if you do. You don't understand. You gotta let us go."

"I'm not letting you go," Gage said. "But tell me who and I'll protect you."

"Even you can't protect us."

"The fish and oyster packing plant in the bay." The man Gage pointed his weapon at swiped blood from his mouth. "Snell owns it. We transport shark fins and drugs. A single fin is worth $50,000. The drugs are more, sure."

"Shut up, Lee!" Charles grabbed Sadie and took the gun, then pressed it to her temple. She was really getting tired of this.

"Now, put down your weapon. Kick it over to me."

Gage slowly placed his gun on the ground and kicked it over.

"I'm so sorry, Gage," she said.

"You have nothing to be sorry about. It's going to be okay. These men don't want to get into more trouble, so they're going to leave us here and make their escape."

Charles laughed. He pointed the gun at Lee and shot him.

The sound startled her and she screamed. "You killed him? You killed your brother? Why?"

"He's not my brother. A distant cousin I never

liked. But he's a talker. He's going to get me killed with his talking, just like he told you way too much already. Now you must die." The evil man grinned. "I have a syringe in my pocket. I'm going to enjoy finally getting to use it on you, but you have to die."

He pointed his weapon.

Gunfire rang out, echoing in her ears again.

The gun slipped from Charles's hand and he fell to the ground, a bullet in his forehead.

Thompkins approached the dead man and dropped to one knee. He felt for a pulse then looked at Gage and shook his head. Right. Like Charles could have lived with a bullet in his head. Gage hadn't even realized Thompkins was approaching, but that had to be on purpose. He hadn't wanted to give himself away too soon.

Gage's knees nearly buckled. "You saved my life. Thank you."

Sadie had crouched next to the other man. He whispered something in her ear. Gage joined her to check the man's wound, but it was no use. The man died right before his eyes. These men could be the only ones who could fully explain the operation and everyone involved with Hank also gone. Regret rolled through him. Had he botched this entire investigation? Someone had to remain alive to answer questions.

But Sadie needed his attention. A tear slid down her cheek. She pushed away from the dead man and stood.

"And my life," she said to Thompkins. "You saved my life too."

Gage rose from the body to face Thompkins. Sadie closed the distance and hugged Gage. He squeezed her to him. Pressed his face into her neck. Closed his eyes as he drew in the scent of her hair. *Thank You, God.*

"Are you all right?" Thompkins asked.

Gage lifted his face. Thompkins arched a brow. Gage hadn't maintained his composure around her in front of Thompkins, but how could he? They'd both almost died.

"Yes. Fine, thanks to you. Your timing couldn't have been better."

A helicopter whirred in the distance. The Coast Guard was on the way. Gage nodded. "Glad you finally made it. What took so long?"

"Your message was garbled on our end. Took us time to figure out what you said. But we finally searched west of where the boat went down in case you swam in. I found the boat at the dock. Couldn't find anyone at the house but found the tunnel. I'm glad I did too. Another thirty seconds and..."

He pursed his lips. Probably didn't want to say anything in front of Sadie.

"What did he whisper to you?" Thompkins asked her.

She pulled from Gage and shrugged. "I asked if they had tried to kill me by leaving me on the boat. He said yes, but with the Coast Guard closing in that day, they called to let you know I needed rescuing."

Gage nodded. "To divert our attention. It worked. We lost them that day, but found and saved you."

"Did he say anything else?"

She shook her head.

Thompkins studied her. "I'm glad this is finally over. I'd appreciate if you'd fill me in on everything before we meet with our SAC."

"Sure thing," Gage said. "But I think I'd like to get Sadie to the hospital first. She's been drugged. The effects have mostly worn off, but I'm worried about her."

Thompkins grinned. "I can see plain enough you're not going to hand her off to someone else."

They followed Thompkins out of the tunnel and back to the staircase to the approaching Coast Guard cutter. Someone called down to them from the top of the stairs. Sheriff Garrison and Deputy Crowley.

"Agent Thompkins? Would you mind if I rode

back with the sheriff?" Sadie asked. "I don't much feel like being on the water again today."

Thompkins chuckled. "No problem. You with me, Gage?"

He angled his head. "I'm with Sadie. I'll call you from the hospital."

"Fair enough." Thompkins descended the stone staircase and headed back to his boat moored at the pier next to the drug runner's go-fast boat and Hank's boat.

After taking their statements, the sheriff and Crowley cordoned off the area as a crime scene, though it was secluded. The sheriff agreed to wait for the coroner and additional deputies as well as the state boys, as he called them.

Crowley drove them back all the way to the Coldwater Bay Hospital. "So Henry Snell III and the Changs are dead? Sean Miller and Karon Casings are dead. Everyone who could tell us anything about this is gone."

"Yep. It appears that way." Gage kept his responses clipped. He held back his true thoughts.

"And I bet you're glad to get back to your life as usual, then, right Miss Strand?"

"Yes, but I… I think I'm starting to remember something. Something more from that first day I went to Karon's house. I think I saw—"

Gage squeezed her hand tight, hoping she understood to keep quiet.

"What's that you say?" Crowley glanced at her through the rearview mirror.

"I was just going to say it won't be the same without Karon. Do you happen to know how her mother is doing?"

"Now that we know something about that drug used, I think the doctors can help her, even though like you said, Mr. Snell said there was no antidote, but we can hope and pray."

Crowley dropped them off at the hospital. "I'm happy to wait with her, Sessions, if you have business to see to in wrapping this up with the Coast Guard."

"I'm sure you have paperwork to do, as well. Including a more detailed statement from me."

The man stared at him. What was it Gage saw in his eyes? Distrust? Fear? Had he heard what Sadie said? "That, I do. Just trying to help."

"Thanks, Crowley, but I'll see to Sadie."

He chuckled. "I thought so. Suit yourself."

Once they had climbed from the vehicle, Gage waved and led Sadie inside the hospital. He pulled her over to the corner.

"What are you doing?" she asked.

"You just told Deputy Crowley you remember something. I don't know who we can trust so I didn't want you to tell him everything."

"What? You don't trust him?"

"I don't know. Tell me what you remember."

"Someone else was there at Karon's house. I always had the sense of someone there, but now I know it wasn't only Hank. Though it's just a shadow in my mind, I think there were two people at Karon's house that day."

Gage raked a hand over his face and scruffy jaw. He needed a doctor to check her out. He needed her to be safe. "Okay, don't tell anyone else what you just told me."

She nodded.

"Let's go see this doctor who is taking care of Donna and knows about the drugs. Get your blood drawn. Get you taken care of." He squeezed her hand again. It was getting to be a habit—the only way he could get closer to her. Closer when he really shouldn't.

A half an hour later, Sadie rested in a hospital bed while they waited for the blood work. Gage stood outside her room waiting on the security detail he'd called in.

The elevator dinged and Jonna Strand strode toward him. Beautiful like her sister Sadie, she was taller and much thinner. "I got your message. What's going on. Why all the secrecy?"

"Sadie is still in danger. I don't know who I can trust to watch over her and keep her safe in the hospital. I have to run an errand."

"You're kidding." She arched a dark brow.

"I'm dead serious." He fisted his hands on his hips. "You were an ICE agent once."

"You're asking me to stand bodyguard over my sister."

"I am."

She rolled her head back, taking in his request, then leveled her gaze on him. "Okay then."

"Don't let anyone take her out of here. Watch everyone like a hawk who goes in to see her—law enforcement included. In fact, maybe say she's resting, but watch medical personnel, as well. And don't scare her, or let her know that I left. I don't want her to try and follow me."

"No, we wouldn't want that, would we?" Amusement danced in her eyes to go with her sarcastic tone, then her features turned somber. "Am I allowed to know what I'm up against?"

"You're up against someone who wants to kill her."

"And you didn't call in actual law enforcement, so that tells me something."

"You're her sister. Nobody will care as much as you."

"Except maybe...you."

EIGHTEEN

Well after dark and the fish and oyster processing plant had closed, Gage stepped inside. The plant supervisor, Gerald Haines, had given him permission to enter and search, and had accompanied him to open up the facility. There'd been no vehicles parked near the plant.

Something clattered in the back.

Gage pulled his weapon out.

"Whoa, what's up with that?" Haines frowned and glanced at Gage.

Gage pressed his fingers to his lips. Haines reached over to flip on the lights.

"Don't," Gage whispered.

"How are you going to see?"

"There's enough lighting in here already. I need to check it out and make sure no one else is here. Where's your office?"

Haines gestured to the right.

"Then get in there and lock yourself in."

Gage ushered the man to his office. Made sure no one else was inside.

"Should I call the sheriff?" Haines asked. "You need backup or something?"

"I'll take care of it. You just lock yourself inside."

The man nodded and did as he was told. Gage hoped his gut was right and the man could be trusted. Gage hated that Haines had to be here because it could be dangerous. When he'd knocked on Haines's door tonight, if the man had told Gage to get a search warrant from a judge, he might have suspected the man involved in the crimes he believed going down at this facility. As it was, he wasn't sure how things could happen without the man knowing. He certainly would have gotten that warrant but it would have taken longer and increased the chances evidence would be moved. But Haines had been nothing if not cooperative.

And as for backup? Gage didn't know who he could trust. Thompkins was supposed to meet him here, and then he could find out the truth from him. Thompkins had been the only one to know they were going to dive for that boat. The idea that he was the inside man turned Gage's insides.

This investigation wasn't over by a long shot. Not with someone else involved.

Gage had to watch his back while he waited for Thompkins. But it was his best chance to get in without tipping off the man he was after. Chances were he had already been tipped off since Gage was closing in on him and he knew it.

Sweat beaded his forehead and soaked the back of his shirt. At least he'd taken a few minutes to change out of the dry suit into something more appropriate for finishing this investigation.

And that's how he saw it too. He would finish it tonight if it killed him.

But he hoped it wouldn't come to that.

Weapon drawn, he crept in through the shadows so he wouldn't be a target. The fact no other vehicles had been parked out front meant nothing. He hoped he was alone here, besides Haines, but he knew his prey would likely anticipate he would come here next. And that was the point, wasn't it? To end this? To find out who was left in this smuggling ring that could continue to harm people? They would kill Sadie once Gage was gone and her guard was down.

He wouldn't leave her until this was over.

His cell buzzed in his pocket. He still hadn't discovered what had made the noise in the back, but he needed Thompkins to be here with him. He eyed the text. Thompkins.

I'M HERE. IT LOOKS DARK IN THERE. YOU OKAY?

Gage texted he'd heard a noise and for Thompkins to come in, but to be careful.

He made his way back up to meet Thompkins. His CGIS counterpart had his weapon drawn, as well.

"Haines is locked in his office. Let's make sure it's safe for him to come out and show us around."

Thompkins nodded. Together he and Thompkins cleared the packing plant in a few minutes.

"Well, looks like no one is here." Thompkins holstered his weapon. "You want me to bring Haines out so he can guide us through the facilities?"

"I'll go with you. Then we'll look for evidence of smuggling. I'm thinking they pack drugs in the crates with fish, stuff it inside them or in the ice. Since they've been processed for now, we might not find what we're looking for, but if we can get something, anything at all, we can confirm what he told us."

"Maybe we need a sting operation. Wait until we catch the workers involved."

Gage nodded. He'd come here to catch only one person tonight. He'd see how it played out.

Together they walked back to the front. "We

can probably switch the lights on too," Gage said. "So we can see better."

"I'm glad you didn't call anyone else for backup, since you don't know who you can trust," Thompkins said.

Acid burned in Gage's gut. "Definitely has to be someone on the inside." Gage hadn't holstered his weapon yet. "Have any idea who that could be?"

Ahead of him, Thompkins shook his head. "You know as much as I do."

"That's right. You have known everything I've known from the start."

Thompkins turned around. "What are you saying? Gage. Are you accusing me?"

Gage held his weapon at low ready, just in case. "You were the only one who knew Sadie and I were diving to find the boat today. You told me not to tell anyone else. That you thought someone was working on the inside. And yet the Changs show up in their boat and try to gun us down. We almost died out there. Someone told them where to find us."

The man didn't react like Gage would expect of a guilty man, but nodded. "I see how that could look suspicious."

"And you were there before anyone else at Hank's house. You took out the only man left who could point you out."

Thompkins shoulders slumped. "Do you even hear yourself? Maybe it's been you this whole time. You're the one on the inside who tipped them off. You're trying to make it look like they're pursuing you so you'll not be a suspect. You brought me here tonight to kill me."

"What? No."

"The truth is you can't prove a thing, Sessions." Thompkins held his hands perfectly still, but ready to pull his weapon in defense. "Or you would have had me arrested already instead of bringing me here tonight. Tipping me off to see if I would move evidence."

"Well? Did you move it?"

Everything pointed to Thompkins. But Gage trusted his gut, if only one more time. Thompkins wasn't his guy. He'd never wanted it to be his counterpart.

"Of course not!" A sadness filled his gaze. "I'm not the person behind this, Gage. But I have my suspicions. I'm thinking it's—"

Gunfire erupted. Thompkins collapsed.

Gage whirled around aiming his weapon and nearly fired.

"Not so fast, Sessions." Crowley held Sadie at gunpoint. "Now, toss your weapon over or your girlfriend dies."

"Gage?" The sound of Sadie's voice was a dagger to his heart.

NINETEEN

This can't be happening!

Sadie struggled against Deputy Crowley's iron grip. "Let me go! What did you do with my sister?"

When the hospital had determined Sadie was going to be okay, they'd released her to go home. Home—where was that? Where could she go to be safe? Jonna had escorted her out of the hospital, intending to take her back to her lodge on the coast and watch over her there. But at her vehicle, someone had hit them both with a Taser gun.

Crowley ignored her question and forced her and Gage into a walk-in freezer, then he hit Gage over the head with his gun, knocking him unconscious. Gage slumped to the floor. Sadie dropped next to him, hating the tears that came. Furious, she shoved to her feet and rushed him. Crowley knocked her down.

"Why? Why are you doing this? How could you?"

She didn't want to die in here. Not this way. But she remembered now. Crowley had knocked her down that day in Karon's house. Though fuzzy, it came back to her in pieces. Crowley had been the other man with Hank at Karon's house that day. If only she could have remembered that sooner. This time she wished he had actually drugged her. She couldn't go through this anymore.

Crowley dragged Gage's unconscious form deeper inside the freezer. He hit Gage with the Taser for good measure.

"Stop it. Just stop it. It's not like he can hurt you!" She hated watching the brutality, seeing Gage unable to defend himself.

There was nothing she could do now. Obviously Crowley had issues with shooting people outright, preferring to have their deaths look like an accident. But he'd shot Thompkins.

Wake up, Gage! Wake up!

"Your boyfriend just couldn't leave it alone. You either. In fact, Hank shouldn't have messed around with Karon and got her suspicious. Everything would be running along smoothly if he hadn't made that one mistake. So she and Sean both had to die because they found out too much, only in a way that it looked like their deaths were unrelated. Karon drowned, and the drug runners killed Sean. I planted the drugs on him so that should have been the end of it. A drug deal gone bad. But no, you just had to show up and start digging too. You should have left her death well enough alone. Because then you and Gage had to die, and you should have gone down with that boat today."

"You! You knew we'd gone out to dive. How? Who told you?"

"I had to keep a close watch on you." He gave her a pitying look. "I knew I was in trouble as soon as you started to remember. You weren't supposed to remember. The Changs were supposed to drown you, to be sure you were dead and leave you on that boat. Hank didn't know what he was talking about on those drugs. They're too risky. Too unpredictable."

"You can't guarantee how anyone will react to them, don't you get it? And that's what makes them all the more dangerous. What's your plan now, Crowley? How do you think you're going to get away with it?"

Crowley rocked his head back then pinned her with his gaze. "Just like Gage suspected, it was Thompkins all along. He had the means and the motive. Anyone has the motive when we're talking this kind of money. I came in to find Thompkins had already dumped you two in the freezer. He tried to shoot me so I shot back. End of story."

Tears slid down her cheeks. She wanted to bring up Jonna. Ask about her sister, but that might endanger her further. Maybe she could escape before Crowley remembered her, if he hadn't already killed her.

"Sleep tight. It won't take long for you to freeze to death. I turned the temperature down. Now… Just go to sleep."

Suddenly Gage scrambled to his feet and rammed into Crowley, knocking him out of the freezer. The door swung open. Sadie stood to her feet and ran out. Gage grabbed Crowley's gun and pressed it against his head.

"Just give me an excuse. You know I'll do it."

Sheriff's deputies and other law enforcement officers suddenly flooded the premises. Sheriff Garrison pulled Gage off Deputy Crowley and started putting handcuffs on Gage.

"Wait, what are you doing?" Sadie asked.

"Sessions attacked me," Crowley said. "He shot Thompkins. I was trying to save the girl."

"Unbelievable," Gage said. "Sheriff, this just isn't true."

Sheriff Garrison grimaced. "We'll sort this out at the station."

"But Gage shouldn't be in cuffs," Sadie pleaded. "Ask Thompkins."

"Unfortunately, he's unconscious."

Sadie feared he'd die in the hospital at the hands of Crowley.

"Why aren't you listening to me?" she asked.

Another man appeared. "She's right, Sheriff. I'm Gerald Haines, the plant supervisor. Your deputy here shot Thompkins and tried to kill these two to cover his involvement in a smuggling ring. It happened right here under my nose and for that I'm ashamed. I had been suspicious for a while and that's when I had called Deputy Crowley in. But I see now he was in on it the whole time."

When the sheriff removed Gage's cuffs and put them on his own deputy, Sadie ran to Gage. She gently touched his bruised and swollen face. "You're still good-looking, even with the bruises."

He laughed then winced. But the way he looked at her, she thought he might kiss her.

"Excuse me. I hate to interrupt you, Sessions." A tall man appeared.

"Agent Finley. It's about time." Gage released Sadie but kept her near as he spoke with the DEA agent.

Jonna jogged up to her. "Sadie!"

"You're okay!" Sadie hugged her sister, letting the tears flow freely. "I was so worried about you."

"He locked me in the trunk of a car. I worked my way out and called the sheriff. But apparently someone had already called them about a disturbance here. They thought you might be involved."

The DEA agent and Gage remained in a long, detailed conversation about the smuggling ring, and Sheriff Garrison joined them.

Another deputy approached Sadie. "I'm Deputy Bree Carrington," she said. "The sheriff wanted me to take your statement about what happened. Are you up for that now?"

Sadie nodded. "Sure, I can do that."

Deputy Carrington had lovely red hair that hung to her shoulders. A soft smile broke through her serious demeanor. "I know your brother."

"Quinn? You know Quinn?"

"I haven't seen him in a while. How is he?"

Sadie slumped. "I can't tell you. We haven't heard from him either. Sometimes I wonder if something happened to him. But I guess he works undercover with the DEA now, and that makes it hard for him to stay in touch."

Deputy Carrington lowered her gaze and nodded as if she understood, but said nothing more. Sadie told the deputy her side of the story while Jonna shared the events of what happened at the hospital. While they held on to each other, supporting each other, it seemed to Sadie that her time with Gage was over. Her reason for being with him had ended.

And once again…the events of life would separate them, and she wasn't sure if she would see Gage after this, which was probably for the best. Because…

Hadn't she sworn off Coasties?

Days later, she walked on the beach, mentally preparing herself to go back to her research. After all, what was left for her here? Her family, sure, but she could come back to see them between projects and on holidays. Aunt Debby had encouraged her to go back and finish her research so she could get her grant. Sadie couldn't change who she was.

Besides, she and Gage had solved Karon's murder and brought down a smuggling ring, which included designer drugs, of all things. Like Hank said, he'd diversified in case something went wrong with one end of his operation, and he had multiple avenues pushing different kinds of drugs. He hadn't counted on things going wrong with both drug venues at the same time. He hadn't counted on Sadie and Gage working together to find the truth. Donna had finally woken up from the drug-induced coma and told them about the email Karon had sent.

In the email she'd written, "Henry Snell III." The email was set to send on a certain date—maybe a way that Karon could communicate should something bad happen to her.

Considering something *had* happened to her daughter, Donna had contacted Crowley about the email after contacting Sadie, and that's why men had descended on her home, drugged her with intent to kill her and took her computer. Karon hadn't known Crowley was involved so hadn't included his name in the email, but it wouldn't take long to link the two if an investigation had been started.

And as for Gage, she hadn't seen him since that night in the fishing plant over a week ago. She wouldn't have thought her heart would ache so much. Karon's murder had brought them together. And there had always been something to keep them apart. This time, she wasn't exactly sure what would keep them apart other than… well…their careers—and that was enough. She had repeatedly told herself she couldn't fall for Gage.

She dropped to her knees and played in the sand.

But I love him…

Why did she always fall for the wrong guy?

Someone plopped down with her in the sand. "Care for some company?"

"Gage? What are you doing here?"

The waves lapped close to them.

"Seeing you? What else should I be doing?"

She grabbed a handful of sand and let it fall through her fingers. "I don't know. Investigating somewhere. Going home to Port Angeles. A million different things you could be doing right now."

"There's only one thing I want to do."

The way he said it made her heart beat erratically. "And what's that?"

She could think of something she wanted to do, as well. But then her heart would be shattered even more.

"A few years ago it ended our friendship. I want to know this time, if it's okay with you if I—"

Sadie didn't wait for him to finish but eased closer and pressed her lips against his. "I hope that's what you were talking about."

He pulled her to him, his hands at her back, and kissed her thoroughly, leaving her breathless, then said, "Yes. I've wanted to kiss you like that for the longest time. Only... I wanted you to *want* my kiss. Want...my love."

"Love?" The word came out husky, and made her heart beat wildly.

"Yes. I love you, Sadie. I think I always have. But you were always into someone else. I tried *not* to love you, I did, but life is too short. I figure life keeps bringing us together and each time, I fall in love with you all over again. I'd rather not have such big gaps between each time I see you…or each time I fall in love with you… if we're destined to run into each other again anyway. I'm just glad I came to my senses before you got away from me again. I'm glad I found you before you left."

He kissed her again and again. Sadie needed to catch her breath. "All right, Special Agent Sessions, what exactly are you trying to say?"

"Marry me?"

She pressed her forehead against his, breathing in his essence. How had she missed loving this man before? They had a lot of lost time to make up for. "Yes, Gage Sessions. Yes. I love you more than life itself. Please, please marry me."

His enticing grin drew her in. "And in the meantime, I can kiss you senseless."

* * * * *

Dear Reader,

I'm so glad you took the time to read *Thread of Revenge*, and I hope you enjoyed the story. As always, I had a lot of fun writing the novel and living my life vicariously through my characters as they tried to survive and solve the puzzle of who was trying to kill them. In my research, this story took me into the dark world of drug smuggling, and into the new and terrifying world of designer drugs, online ordering of those drugs, along with postal service delivery. Writing stories like this can often leave me concerned about the world we live in, and for my children's future, but I have to remind myself that God is with me. He will never leave nor forsake me. And I know that to be true.

I pray for His wisdom and guidance in your life, and that you'll know without a doubt that He's with you, even when you're struggling through the darkest of times. I pray His many blessings on you, my friend.

If you'd like to know more about me or my books, please connect with me at my website: ElizabethGoddard.com. You can find my Facebook and Twitter pages there too. I hope to hear from you soon!

Blessings!
Elizabeth Goddard

Get 2 Free Books,
Plus 2 Free Gifts—
just for trying the Reader Service!

Get 2 Free Books,
Plus 2 Free Gifts —
just for trying the Reader Service!

Get 2 Free Books,

Plus 2 Free Gifts—
just for trying the
Reader Service!

HOME *on the* RANCH

Get 2 Free Books,
Plus 2 Free Gifts -
just for trying the Reader Service!

STRS17R2